"Zach, I'm Not Ready For A Personal Commitment," TJ Explained.

"We have to talk about it," he said quietly.

"I'm not against discussion, but I'm very confused right now." Being in his arms was clouding her mind.

"If we can't talk, can we do this?" His mouth touched hers, sending a shock wave through her that resulted in a head-to-toe shiver. "I'm burning up for you, TJ."

She was burning, too. Every cell of her body felt like it was on fire. Zach looked deeply into her eyes. "Kiss me," he whispered. "The way you want to, the way I want you to. It's not a crime to want someone. Stop denying it or wishing it out of existence. It's not going to go away—not my feelings, not yours."

Everything female in TJ seemed to magnify in response. Her hands locked behind Zach's head, and she placed her lips on his....

Dear Reader,

April is here and spring is in the air! But if you aren't one of those lucky people who gets to spend April in Paris, you can still take that trip to romance—with Silhouette Desire!

You can fly off to San Francisco—one of *my* favorite cities!—and meet Frank Chambers, April's *Man of the Month,* in *Dream Mender* by Sherryl Woods. Or you can get into a car and trek across America with Brooke Ferguson and Pete Cooper in *Isn't It Romantic?* by Kathleen Korbel. (No, I'm not going to tell you what Pete and Brooke are doing. You have to read the book!) And if you're feeling particularly adventurous, you can battle fish, mud and flood with Dom Seeger and Alicia Bernard in Karen Leabo's delightful *Unearthly Delights.*

Of course, we all know that you don't *have* to travel to find love. Sometimes happiness is in your own backyard. In Jackie Merritt's *Boss Lady,* very desperate and very pregnant TJ Reese meets hometown hunk Marc Torelli. Tricia Everett finds that the man of her dreams is . . . her husband, in Noelle Berry McCue's *Moonlight Promise.* And Caroline Nobel returns to the man who's always lit her fire in *Hometown Man* by Jo Ann Algermissen.

So, it might not be April in Paris for you—*this* year. But don't worry, it's still love—at home or away— with Silhouette Desire.

Until next month,

Lucia Macro
Senior Editor

JACKIE MERRITT

BOSS LADY

SILHOUETTE *Desire*®

Published by Silhouette Books New York

America's Publisher of Contemporary Romance

SILHOUETTE BOOKS
300 East 42nd St., New York, N.Y. 10017

BOSS LADY

Copyright © 1992 by Carolyn Joyner

All rights reserved. Except for use in any review, the reproduction or utilization of this work in whole or in part in any form by any electronic, mechanical or other means, now known or hereafter invented, including xerography, photocopying and recording, or in any information storage or retrieval system, is forbidden without the permission of the publisher, Silhouette Books, 300 E. 42nd St., New York, N.Y. 10017

ISBN: 0-373-05705-9

First Silhouette Books printing April 1992

All the characters in this book have no existence outside the imagination of the author and have no relation whatsoever to anyone bearing the same name or names. They are not even distantly inspired by any individual known or unknown to the author, and all incidents are pure invention.

® and ™: Trademarks used with authorization. Trademarks indicated with ® are registered in the United States Patent and Trademark Office, the Canada Trade Mark Office and in other countries.

Printed in the U.S.A.

JACKIE MERRITT

and her husband live just outside of Las Vegas, Nevada. An accountant for many years, Jackie has happily traded numbers for words. Next to family, books are her greatest joy, both for reading and writing.

One

Employment Opportunity
Qualified person needed for supervision and coor-
dination of construction crews and subcontractors.
Must have experience in overseeing all phases of sin-
gle-family home construction. Contact TJ Reese Home
Builders, 555-3333, 4304 Morrow Lane, Las Vegas, NV.
We are an Equal Opportunity Employer.

Zach Torelli read the ad a second and then a third time. In Las Vegas's busy construction community, Reese Home Builders had a good reputation. With his eyes narrowed thoughtfully, Zach tried to call up an elusive memory.

He snapped his fingers. Tommy Reese! Yes, that was it. He'd met Tommy several years back, while Vista Construction Company, Zach's own business, had been flying high. Zach's expression became brooding. Vista was a thing of the past, flat on its butt in the Vegas dust instead of soaring among the glitz and glamour of the valley as it had once been.

And he needed a job. Zach glanced at the ad again. Maybe Tommy Reese would remember him. But he wouldn't use that telephone number. Seeing Tommy in person would be a much better reminder of the days when the names "Torelli" and "Vista" meant something. He could explain what happened to his company—although the whole mess had been splattered across the daily newspapers—and if he recalled Tommy Reese correctly from that one brief meeting, he would be dealing with a gregarious, slap-on-the-back sort of guy.

A frown appeared. Tommy hadn't been alone when they'd been introduced. A woman had been hanging on his arm. Zach had been with three other men—out-of-town investors—showing them a good time in Vegas. They'd been walking through Caesars Palace, and one of the men had known Tommy.

The memory wasn't very clear to Zach. He couldn't remember whether the woman had been Tommy's wife or girlfriend. He shrugged. It probably didn't matter. He would be applying for a job, not a membership into Tommy Reese's circle of friends.

What went up sometimes came down fast and didn't stop falling until it hit bedrock, and that's where Zach was right now, at the bottom. The demise of his company had been a nightmare of accountants and attorneys and finally a stunning realization that he had been taken by a man he had thoroughly trusted, Vincent Torelli, his only living relative, a cousin.

It didn't make Zach sick to his stomach to think about the past year's overwhelming trauma any longer, although they had been hellish months to live through. These days his thoughts were determined again. It might be a kick in the ego to draw a paycheck instead of owning the company, but he had to earn a living. And he'd operate his own company again, if he had to work day and night until he acquired the means to start over.

Tearing the page of want ads free from the newspaper, Zach encircled the Reese ad with a red marker, then folded the sheet into a neat little square. Tucking it into his shirt pocket, he went to the bathroom of his modest apartment, brushed his hair and checked out his jeans and off-white shirt in the mirror.

Dark hair and blue eyes reflected back at him. He was a long ways from the tastefully dressed, successful business-man Tommy Reese had met in Caesars Palace. But then, Tommy might not even remember the incident.

Leaving the apartment, Zach got in his Wagoneer and began the drive across town. Starting over, beginning at square one again felt oddly exciting. This time he would make no mistakes—or, at least, not the same kind.

Holding her hand to the dull ache in the small of her back, TJ Reese stood at the large window in the north wall of her office. Outside, everything in sight—cacti, ficus trees, parked cars, asphalt—shimmered in the 103-degree heat. Only a week ago the thermometer had read 112 and up-ward at this time of day. TJ smiled with vague amusement; Las Vegas was beginning to cool off.

A glance over her shoulder to her desk calendar chased TJ's smile. It was the twentieth of August and she was starting her ninth month of pregnancy. Her calculations were scrupulously accurate; few mothers-to-be had the kind of signposts that she did.

Sighing, TJ sat behind her desk and began clearing it of papers, pens and odds and ends. It was nearly six and time to go home for the day. She was almost the last one to leave, which was normal. One man remained in a back office, Jim Cope, her accountant. Office hours were eight to five, but TJ usually liked a breather after her secretary, Doreen, had gone, the phones had stopped ringing and employees and subcontractors had ceased trooping in and out.

A cool bath and a cold drink—nonalcoholic—awaited her at home, and she was tired and ready to brave the heat dur-ing the drive. The air-conditioned car would cool down af-ter a few blocks, although it would feel like a blast furnace when she first got into it.

Touching her rounded tummy, TJ smiled again. It *was* cooling down, and September was normally a beautiful month in southern Nevada, a great time of year to have a baby. Granted, the child would be a mixed blessing, but common sense worries simply could not dull the joy of impending motherhood, no matter how dire they seemed at times.

The sound of the small building's outside door opening brought TJ's eyes to her office door, which, as usual, was wide open. "In here," she called out.

The outside door closed, and footsteps echoed from the parquet flooring of the foyer. A tall, dark-haired man appeared in TJ's doorway.

Zach stopped. Traffic across the city had been horrific, holding him up again and again. He lived on the west side, and Reese Home Builders' office was on the east. Unfamiliar with the area, it had taken him a few minutes to locate Morrow Lane. The delays had added up, and he was here later than he should be. It was obvious from the silence in the building that the workday was over; only one woman was still here.

He glanced down at the square of newspaper, then back to the woman. "I'll come back tomorrow. I'm looking for..." he used the name in the ad rather than "Tommy" "...TJ Reese."

TJ looked the man over. Inches over six feet tall, well built, a handsome face and thick, dark hair. Expensive jeans, shirt and cowboy boots. Hmm.

"Are you here about my ad?" she asked, a little skeptical about the possibility, although she was fairly certain he was holding a section of newspaper. First impressions could be terribly deceiving, but this man didn't strike her as your average, everyday construction worker.

"*Your* ad?"

"Yes, my ad for a super."

Zach cleared his throat. "It says to contact TJ Reese."

"Yes, I know. I'm TJ."

Questions about the accuracy of his own memory flicked through Zach's mind. He'd been so sure about meeting Tommy Reese that one time, and then "TJ" had connected with the name "Tommy," and...

Well, he'd apparently been mistaken. Maybe the Tommy Reese he remembered hadn't even been associated with this company. Something didn't add up, but there was little to be gained from standing here and trying to figure it out.

He moved into the room. "I'm Zach Torelli. If that job's still open, I'd like to fill out an application."

TJ nodded. "It's still open, Mr. Torelli. Please sit down." She gestured to the two chairs at the front of her desk.

"Thanks." Zach approached the chairs and chose the one on the right. The lady across the desk had a direct gaze and she was sizing him up. He sat very still and let her have her look, but also used the opportunity to take a look of his own. TJ's dark blond hair was drawn away from her face and to the back of her head by something he couldn't see, a clasp probably. She wore very little, if any, makeup, although cosmetics would likely make her pretty face beautiful. She had a great mouth—sensual and femininely shaped—and gray green, intelligent eyes that looked tired.

Her white blouse or dress top, whichever it was, had a rounded neckline and appeared to be a plainly designed cotton garment, sensible attire in this weather, but almost sexless in its austerity. All in all, she appeared to be a no-nonsense, all-business sort of woman.

"Before we get to the application, Mr. Torelli, I would like to stress exactly what it is I'm looking for in a superintendent."

"Fine," he replied agreeably, understanding what she didn't say: *If you don't have the qualifications, please don't waste my time with an application.*

"I've reached the point of bluntness, so please don't take anything I say as personal. In the past seven months I've hired and fired four different supervisors. I need someone who understands both blueprints and subcontractors, no small talent, I've discovered. I will not tolerate dishonesty in any form, which was the case with two of my former supers. I requested experience in my ad, and I probably should have indicated at least several *years'* experience. I want someone who will be on the job every single workday, and not shut everything down because one cloud passes overhead and the crew does a rain dance.''

Zach laughed softly. He knew the local contractors' routine with rain. Up North, construction went on through rain, sleet and snow, but in the Southwest, with the first threat of a sprinkle, everyone yelled "danger" because of electrically powered tools.

Of course, when it really *did* rain in the Vegas valley or surrounding mountains, it was no laughing matter. Flash flooding inundated streets and snarled an already congested and increasingly inadequate road system. With the population growing at the rate of four to six thousand people a month, schools, roads and utilities were feeling the effects.

But that tremendous growth was what made the construction business so lucrative, too. Experts predicted the boom would last another decade, an opinion with which Zach fully agreed. Legalized gambling and enormous hotel-casinos, each one employing thousands of people, were the big draw, of course, although other industries were beginning to see the value of southern Nevada's dry desert climate and rapidly expanding work force.

The man's brief but pleasant laugh had brought a smile to TJ's lips. "Are you from Las Vegas, Mr. Torelli?"

He smiled rather wryly. "Is anyone?"

"You're right, of course. Vegas has very few natives. The area is growing so fast, almost everyone you meet is from somewhere else."

"Where are you from?"

"California."

"I came here from New York twelve years ago," he said.

"Oh, well, you're *almost* a native, aren't you?" The man sitting across her desk was maybe the best-looking one she'd ever met. His smile showed bright white teeth and crinkled the corners of his vivid blue eyes. Somehow the name "Torelli" and blue eyes didn't quite jibe in TJ's mind, but there they were, right in front of her. Torelli's skin was as Italian as his name, though, dark and smooth as rich honey.

Well, he knew what she wanted in a superintendent. At this point there was nothing for her to do but give him the application form.

Reaching into a lower desk drawer, TJ took out one of the standard forms. "Go ahead and fill this out," she said, passing the paper to Zach's outstretched hand. "You can sit at that table over there."

"Thanks." Getting to his feet, Zach crossed the room to the table and sat down again. Using his own gold pen, he started filling in blanks.

TJ finished clearing her desk, then, just in case Zach Torelli had the right experience, she got out her own personal files on the company's current projects, readying them for discussion. She desperately needed a good supervisor. She was at a stage of her pregnancy where running around from one project to another in the heat was getting her down. The activity hadn't hurt her physically. To the contrary, she hadn't gained an ounce over her doctor's recommendation and was in excellent health. But the eighteen pounds around her middle were becoming cumbersome and tiring. Some days she wished she could stay home with her feet up instead of going to work at all.

But this business was her living, her future, and the baby's, too. And she was going to be a single parent, the sole support of the small life she was carrying under her heart. There were moments when her own private reality was tough to face, nights when she still wept after eight months of trying to understand the man she had been married to for six years and then lost in a senseless, drunken car accident.

That wasn't altogether true. She had lost Tommy long before that accident. They had both known for some time that their marriage was a dead issue and that the only thing keeping them together was the business.

This business.

The subject never failed to unsettle TJ, and she put it out of her mind. She had learned that she was pregnant only weeks after Tommy's funeral, and wondering if maybe the baby coming might have reunited her and Tommy was an exercise in futility.

Her gaze wandered over to Zach Torelli. She had received three other responses to her current want ad, with none of the applicants worth a darn. Good supers were not out of work in the construction business, and she was weary of trying to get by with less than adequate help. As she had told Mr. Torelli, she had hired and fired four different candidates within the past seven months. If she didn't find a capable assistant soon, she was going to be in very big trouble.

Zach glanced up to see TJ Reese's large, gray green eyes on him. She actually *hoped* he could fill the job, he realized, which gave him hope, too. She was a nice lady, and he sure did need a good job.

Returning his attention to the form, questions darted through his mind. Did TJ own this company all by herself? Was there some connection between her and the Tommy Reese he remembered?

And then a possibility struck him. Maybe she was Tommy's wife! After all, that meeting had occurred several years ago, and the woman draped on Tommy could have been someone he'd known before his marriage even took place.

Completing the form, Zach returned his pen to his shirt pocket and stood up. He walked to TJ's desk and laid the form on it. "All finished. Shall I check with you, or will you call me?"

TJ picked up the form. "I'll call you, Mr. Torelli, one way or the other."

"Thanks." He was almost to the door when he heard, "Mr. Torelli?" He stopped and turned. "Yes?"

"It says here that you hold a general contractor's license."

"I do."

"But..." TJ was reading. "Oh, I see. You operated your own company for ten years, Vista Constr...oh!"

"You heard about it, apparently."

"Of course. Vegas isn't that big when it comes right down to it, is it? And your...family problems were in the newspapers." TJ's expression contained compassion. "Now I recognize your name. I'm sorry."

He found a faint, somewhat cynical grin. "So am I. It was a good company."

"Please...sit down." TJ's heart was beating abnormally fast. This man could be the answer to her prayers. He'd been in the business for years, and as crass as it might be, his misfortune could be her *good* fortune.

Zach sat down. There was something funny here. TJ Reese needed him...or someone like him, badly. And if she looked at the arrangement as opportune, it was no more than he was doing. An experienced super earned good money, which he had to have if he was ever going to get another company of his own off the ground.

Which was an extremely important aspect of the job. "What are you paying?" he asked quietly.

TJ looked up at Torelli and carefully chose her words. "The going rate plus a bonus of five percent on every house brought in on time."

"Five percent of the gross?"

She smiled knowingly. "Five percent of the net."

"Excluding office overhead?"

TJ hesitated. He was asking for a very big concession, an extremely shrewd move on his part. Administrative overhead could eat up profits, which anyone who had ever owned and operated a business knew very well. Using Torelli's figures, she would be paying him between two and three thousand dollars a week, but in her present situation company profits were in jeopardy anyway. It was better to be generous than to face the next few months alone.

Their gazes met and held across the desk. He had remarkably eyes, a true unabashed blue. His self-confidence came through loud and clear. He seemed to have no doubt that he could handle the job, and wasn't that what she wanted in a supervisor, a man with confidence in is own ability?

"Very well," she finally agreed.

Zach exhaled, a satisfied sound. "I can start in the morning."

Relief of such magnitude washed through TJ, she only then realized how tense she really had been. The relief could be premature, she knew. Years of experience, his own contractor's license, understanding the pressure of operating a business and even supreme confidence didn't guarantee a man's stability. "Before we shake hands, Mr. Torelli, let me clarify a few points. I'm willing to pay an unusually high salary because I expect a lot in return. If the subcontractors work on weekends, which happens fairly regularly, I will want you on the job."

"Working weekends won't be any kind of hardship."

Ignoring the hopefully excited pulsing of her system, TJ continued. "We're talking very long days and tremendous responsibility."

Zach nodded slowly. "I understand."

TJ again looked at the application, which was glaringly devoid of personal information. She believed totally in equality between the sexes in job placement, and anyone, whatever race, color or creed, had the same chance of getting the super's job as Zach Torelli did. Her requirements were completely unbiased. Knowledge, experience and a person of good conscience were really all she asked for in any employee.

But sometimes the current application forms were frustrating. She had to guess at Zach Torelli's age, and there was no place to indicate family affiliation. Technically she shouldn't ask a possible employee personally slanted questions, like, "Do you have a wife and children?"

She did have questions, though. Zach, sitting there with a passive expression that concealed his elation, began to get the drift of TJ's hesitancy. He shifted slightly in his chair. "Nothing will interfere with the job. Right now I'm renting an apartment on the west side of town, but I'll find something over here by the end of the month. I have no family and moving isn't a problem."

TJ's eyes lifted with some gratitude. In a few sentences he had cleared up most of her concerns. She didn't want to appear overly picky, but she really was in desperate need of a conscientious, dedicated superintendent. As selfish as the attitude probably was, she was glad he didn't have a family and was mobile enough to move to her side of town.

Maybe he was too good to be true, TJ thought with an inward sigh. But right at the moment she was thrilled to give him a chance. Inviting a handshake by extending her hand, TJ started to get to her feet. But Zach beat her to it and stood over the desk, holding her hand in a clasp that signified an agreement reached.

"Thanks," he said softly. "You won't regret hiring me."

His hand was big and warm and felt like a connection with solid security. TJ admitted the undeniable but unusual sensation, as fleeting as it was. Their hands separated and Zach continued to stand there. "I'd like to take a look at your projects yet this evening."

Her load was shifting to his broad shoulders already. Pleased that he was so eager to get started, TJ picked up the four file folders from the desk. "Take these, but please return them in the morning. They're my own notations on the current projects. More detailed files are available, of course, but these will give you addresses and a preliminary feel for what's going on."

"Great."

"The crews start working at six in the morning. Why don't you meet me here around six and we'll visit the sites together."

"I'll be here. See you then."

TJ watched her new employee stroll out of her office, then listened to his footsteps in the foyer. The building's outer door opened and closed, and then the distant sound of a car starting up and driving away put a finality to the interview.

She sat back in her chair and breathed a big sigh of unrestrained relief. At long last her quest for a top-notch supervisor was over. Intuition, as well as facts, told her that Zach Torelli was perfect for the job.

For one thing, his honesty had been well touted by the media. TJ thought about the news coverage of Vincent Torelli's trial and ultimate conviction. It had been proved that Zach's cousin had not only stolen from him, he had embezzled money slated for taxes and defrauded several banks, bankrupting Vista Construction in the process. The money had been irretrievable as Vincent had gambled it away. Zach's name had been totally cleared; his only crime had been in putting too much trust in Vincent.

What a terrible thing to go through. Frowning, TJ felt the anguish of misplaced trust in her own soul, a feeling not unlike some she had endured with Tommy. Not that Tommy had been intrinsically dishonest. But he hadn't handled success and a good income well. Money in his pocket had seemed to alter his personal values, especially his sense of marital fidelity.

TJ laid a protective hand on her distended stomach. The baby had been conceived one night after months of her and Tommy using separate bedrooms. She had become frightened by the coldness between them, and had made one more attempt to get Tommy to see what he was doing to their marriage.

With candlelight and wine, she had wooed her own husband into bed, but the seduction hadn't worked. The very next night he'd come home late, reeking of another woman's perfume.

They began talking about divorce and how to divide up their assets, no small matter. They had both worked hard to build up the business, and neither wanted to walk away from it. The problem disappeared with Tommy's death, a tragic conclusion to six years of marriage.

Engrossed, TJ jumped when Jim Cope appeared in the doorway. "I'm leaving now, TJ. You should go home, too."

"I am, Jim, thanks." Pushing her chair back, TJ gave herself a heave up to her feet. "By the way, I hired another supervisor, only a few minutes ago."

The middle-aged, graying man grinned. "We'll keep our fingers crossed, right?"

TJ grinned back. "Right."

"Come on, I'll walk out with you."

Jim Cope, a widower, was like a mother hen to TJ. So was Doreen, her secretary, for that matter. But Doreen had kids and had to leave right at five every day. Jim had never said so, but TJ suspected he deliberately worked past five because she did.

They locked up and walked out into the heat. Jim saw her to her car, which TJ started immediately. "See you tomorrow, Jim," she called as he closed her door.

Zach Torelli was in her mind during the drive home, but it wasn't until she was turning into her driveway that a strange thought came to TJ. She had remained behind her desk during the entire interview, and it was quite likely Zach Torelli didn't know that his lady boss was pregnant.

Two

It was nearly dark when Zach reached the west side of the city. He had located and stopped at all four of Reese Home Builders' current projects, which encompassed thirty-two tract houses in one phase of a development, thirty-two in a second phase, and some miles away, two quite spectacular custom homes, all of which were in various stages of construction. A few blocks away from his apartment complex, Zach pulled into the parking lot of a moderately priced restaurant and went in to have dinner.

After ordering, he sipped coffee and enjoyed the exultation blooming within him. Landing a good job had definitely made his day. The bonus arrangement he had requested would mean impressive paychecks, which were exactly what he needed to get another business of his own off the ground. What's more, his position with Reese would enable him to keep costs down and increase the company's profits, which, in turn, would increase his own take-home pay. But he would earn every penny he was paid. He had never been afraid of hard work, only too damned trusting, a mistake he wouldn't repeat in the future.

Actually, Zach felt that the experience with Vincent had wised him up to the ways of the business world. If a man couldn't trust his own blood relative, who could he trust? Even at that, the thought of his cousin in prison was horrifying. And it hadn't been Zach's doing, either. He probably never would have pressed embezzlement charges, but once the federal tax people and a couple of banks got involved, the matter had been whisked out of his hands and into the judicial system so fast, it had made his head spin.

It didn't surprise Zach that TJ Reese had heard about the mess. Everyone in Vegas who read the newspapers or watched television newscasts had been exposed to it for several months.

Thinking of TJ raised questions about Tommy again. Was there a connection between the two "Reeses"? And if so, why had TJ seemed so desperately in need of a super? In other words, where was Tommy?

Continuing to mull it over while he ate, Zach decided to do a little investigating. He had friends who might know the Reeses' backgrounds, although it was no secret that quite a few so-called friends had become unreachable during Vincent's trial. That was probably only a predictable side effect of so much adverse publicity, and Zach had come to accept it. The people who were still friends had obviously been his *only* friends.

When he got to his apartment, he sat down by the telephone and dialed a number, which was answered after the third ring. After exchanging hellos and a few joking comments with his friend, Carl Oakland, Zach mentioned Reese Home Builders. "I'll be starting as their new super in the morning."

Carl was enthusiastic. "Hey, that's great, man!"

"Carl, I'm just a little bit confused. Did you ever meet Tommy Reese?"

"Sure. He was a pretty good guy."

"Was?"

"Hell, he died about…let me see…must be seven, eight months ago. Maybe longer than that."

Zach's voice got very quiet. "Did he have a wife?"

"I'm not sure, Zach. Why?"

For some reason Zach was reluctant to bring up TJ's name. "No reason. What happened to Tommy?"

"Car accident. Say, I remember now that a woman was in that accident with him. Maybe she was his wife."

"Maybe," Zach agreed speculatively. "I guess I was so involved with my own problems at the time, Tommy's death went right over my head."

"It's understandable, Zach. You had your hands full."

"Yeah, I did." Knowing how true that was didn't alleviate a certain amount of guilt for Zach. Sure, he'd had his hands full, but blocking out everything else going on seemed pretty self-centered, all the same. "This company I'm going to work for, Reese Home Builders—that was Tommy's company, wasn't it?"

"Sure was. You know, now that I think about it, I'm pretty sure Tommy did have a wife. I remember hearing something about him having a lady contractor in the family. I wonder if she *was* the woman in that accident."

Zach wondered, too. The hope he'd sensed from TJ made sense now. With Tommy dead, she was running that business all by herself.

After signing off with Carl, Zach sat back and frowned at his boots. He would do the best job possible for TJ, but eventually he wanted to be in business for himself again. Maybe he should explain that to her.

Early mornings were gorgeous in the Vegas Valley, no matter how hot it got later in the day. At five-thirty TJ drove to the office, feeling as if a ten-ton burden had disappeared. She had slept wonderfully well and felt chipper and refreshed. Zach Torelli was a godsend. She would spend whatever time it took to pass on the company's policies and methods to her new super, but then everything would change. She would have time to relax and to make plans for the baby.

Smiling, TJ pulled into the parking lot. The early-morning quiet was lovely, peaceful, and she unlocked and went into the silent office building with a sense of relaxed anticipation. She puttered in her own office while she awaited Torelli's arrival, small tasks that required little thought.

And then she heard the sound of a vehicle out front. TJ took a deep breath. Envisioning the next few minutes was immediately unsettling. It was a sensation that she'd refused to contemplate before this, although now she had to admit it had been lurking in her system since yesterday afternoon.

Not that she was thinking of Zach Torelli as anything beyond an employee—a *valued* employee, she ardently hoped—but exposing her obviously pregnant self to his eyes touched on something almost intimate, a far cry from the pride she normally felt about her condition.

Maybe it had something to do with his good looks, TJ told herself, although that explanation seemed uncomfortably shallow. What did a man's looks have to do with anything? Did a handsome face and a long, lanky body guarantee intelligence? An ability to direct construction crews and subcontractors? That took talent, not looks. She believed Zach had that talent, but only time would prove her right or wrong.

With a solid determination to vanquish any female foolishness she might develop around her new supervisor, TJ stood up and deliberately walked around her desk. Zach would get the complete picture without fanfare or delay, which was exactly how she wanted it.

Zach stopped at the door. TJ was wearing pink today, he noticed, and wasn't very tall. His gaze dropped then, and when it reached her waistline, TJ saw comprehension strike Zach Torelli right between the eyes.

What TJ couldn't see was the sudden sharp ache in the pit of Zach's stomach. An unforeseen blow couldn't have surprised him any more than his lady boss's advanced pregnancy. Yesterday he'd suspected nothing and this morning he knew why. TJ was slender except for a basketball-size tummy. Her arms, shoulders, throat and face didn't advertise her condition, and that's all he had seen of her. Other than a nicely rounded bosom, which he'd had no business even noticing.

She suddenly seemed prettier, softer, more feminine to Zach. He cleared his throat, and TJ rushed to dispel his discomfort. "I realized after you left that I should have said something about this." Her hand rose to her abdomen and their gazes tangled over the gesture.

"When is the baby due?"

"The twentieth of September."

"Which is why you needed a super so badly."

"I should have explained."

Zach looked away from the kindly light in her eyes. He could really like this woman, and the gut feeling was all mixed up with the death of her husband and her pregnancy. Everyone had troubles, Lord knows he'd had his share. But there was something touchingly courageous about a pregnant woman trying to keep everything going without a man at her side.

"I met Tommy once," he said quietly.

TJ hadn't expected that comment, and as usually happened when someone mentioned the past, her emotions withdrew into a self-protective shell. "Tommy knew a lot of people," she said coolly. "He got around."

Zach's eyes jerked back to her. Her tone of voice had changed completely, implying his intrusion on personal ground. "Sorry," he said quickly.

TJ moved around her desk with a remote expression. "Did you locate the projects last night?"

"Yes. I have your files right here." Zach walked to her desk and laid the files on it with a frown. Mentioning Tommy had been some kind of blunder, which made little sense. Unless TJ's feelings were still so raw about her husband's death she couldn't bear to hear his name.

Still, her remarks had sounded more defensive than grief stricken.

TJ sat down. It stung her pride that Zach Torelli had known Tommy, which meant, undoubtedly, that he also knew about Tommy's reputation.

It happened all the time. Some new subcontractor or carpenter would come along and announce an old friendship with Tommy, and TJ would see right in the man's eyes that Tommy Reese had been hell on wheels with the ladies. It was a sick sort of macho pride, as though one man's sexual prowess made the entire gender more masculine.

Sometimes TJ saw and felt a newcomer's pity, though, which was worse. Pity made her sick to her stomach. She might have deserved pity when Tommy was alive and running around with anything in skirts, but not now. Not when she was successful in a male-dominated field and holding her own emotionally.

Well, she was, she thought defiantly, ready to defend her emotional state even to herself. A sporadic bout of tears was only normal in a pregnant woman, wasn't it?

Besides, those weepy spells were few and far between and never, never in front of anyone else.

"Let's talk about policy," she said, her tone putting her and Zach on a strictly employer-employee basis. "We'll go over the projects, also, and then take a drive to each job site so I can introduce you to the company crew members."

"Whatever you say," Zach replied evenly. However TJ wanted their relationship was how it would be. Sometimes it was best if a boss remained distanced from his—*her*—employees, anyway.

Glancing at her watch, TJ blinked in amazement. She'd rambled for nearly two hours? Doreen would be arriving any minute, and she had already introduced Jim Cope and his computer whiz of an assistant to Zach Torelli as, one at a time, they had passed by her office door.

This much-too-long conversation was Zach's fault, TJ decided. He was not only a good listener—and she really did enjoy talking about the business—but he had asked intelligent, pertinent questions, which had prodded her on.

"Well, you know almost as much about this place as I do," she quipped as she got to her feet.

Once they had started talking, TJ seemed to have forgotten his reference to Tommy, Zach had noted, making himself a promise to stay out of her personal life. She was a pleasure to talk to, a really aware lady with a genuine grasp of the construction business.

Rising, Zach tore off the sheets of a yellow pad that he'd used for some notes, folded them and slipped them into the back pocket of his jeans.

TJ headed for the door. "Let's leave before this place gets all stirred up for the day."

"Maybe I should take my own car," Zach suggested, following her out.

"Let's ride together this time. You can pick up your car later on and return to whichever job needs your attention."

"All right."

Just as they were getting in TJ's car, a compact red sedan pulled into the lot. "Oh, there's Doreen. Let me introduce you two before we leave," TJ exclaimed.

Zach came around the front of TJ's white Mercedes, admiring the elegant car while Doreen scrambled out of hers. His own luxury car had been swallowed up in the bankruptcy, but he planned on owning another one someday. Right now he felt fortunate to have a three-year-old Wagoneer. At least it was paid for and dependable.

"Morning, TJ," the woman called.

"Come and meet our new super, Doreen."

Zach turned his gaze to the woman tripping across the asphalt on very high heels. She was about thirty—around TJ's age—he figured, and cute. Yes, that was the word. The woman was small and perky-looking, with a bright smile and friendly blue eyes. Her light brown hair was spirally curled, framing a gamine face.

"Doreen Potter, Zach Torelli. Doreen's my secretary, Zach, and she's almost as necessary as my right hand."

"The new super, hmm?" Doreen held out her hand with a big smile. "Nice meeting you."

"My pleasure," Zach replied over the handshake. TJ had some darned good help, if personality and sincerity counted. The three people he'd met so far cared for their boss in a very *un*businesslike way, which felt good to Zach. He realized that he was deep-down glad that TJ had *someone* caring about her.

TJ sensed the intense scrutiny Doreen's warm smile of welcome was disguising. She was weighing and measuring Zach Torelli, and TJ knew that at the first opportunity, Doreen would pass on her opinion in no uncertain terms.

Well, even Doreen's extracritical eye wouldn't be able to find very much wrong with the new super's appearance. The man was almost too good-looking to be believed. Although, from experience, TJ knew that Doreen ordinarily skipped past exteriors and went right for the heart of a person. Doreen was a happily married woman with two great kids, and good-looking men didn't fluster her in the least.

TJ spoke of her immediate plans. "We're going out to each of the job sites. I should be back no later than noon."

Doreen acknowledged the information with a nod and turned back to Zach. "Welcome to the company, Zach. If you need my assistance with anything, just yell out."

"Thanks, I will."

Jim Cope had also been cordial, and Zach knew that Jim and Doreen were probably TJ's most important employees. Not that the construction crews weren't crucial to the company, but good, honest, loyal administrative help was the backbone of any company. Who knew that better than Zach Torelli?

His expression wry, Zach opened the driver's door for TJ. "Thanks," she responded. Her slide beneath the wheel wasn't altogether graceful, but her tummy seemed to be getting in the way lately. During the next month, TJ suspected, she could very well learn what the word *awkward* really meant.

Zach jogged around the front of the car with an enviable agility and got in while TJ started the engine. She paused then to fasten her seat belt, giving Zach a silent directive that made him grin and fasten his own safety belt.

Then they were off. TJ talked while she drove, pointing out various housing developments, some of which Reese Home Builders had worked on. "What I attempt to obtain with a developer is an overall contract, Zach, even though I have to turn around and sub out the electrical, the plumbing and several other phases of construction. Quality control," TJ emphatically declared. "That's what earns a reputation, and that's what we do our best to maintain."

This was ground already covered during the two-hour conversation in TJ's office, but Zach nodded agreeably.

"Jim is very good with bids. Once a job is laid out, he contacts half a dozen electrical contractors, for example, and requests price bids. We don't always choose the lowest, because, as I'm sure you know from your own company, you get what pay for. Sometimes a few hundred dollars is the only difference between a substandard job and one that adds real value to the project."

Listening and agreeing with TJ was about all he could do on his first day on the job. Tomorrow, or sometime in the future, he might have a few ideas of his own, which wouldn't necessarily coincide with hers. When that happened he would speak up. For now, Zach was satisfied to let TJ do most of the talking.

Besides, there was one topic he hadn't brought up, and it was prowling his system like something sinister—his plan to operate his own business again. Somehow it didn't feel right to bring it up today, although he had intended doing exactly that. TJ's enthusiasm, along with the discovery that she was going to have a baby in only one more month, made a reference to quitting the job he had just begun seem almost traitorous.

The woman was pregnant and widowed, a hell of a situation for anyone to be in. Realizing that he should have made his own plans very clear yesterday, long before they had shaken hands on the job, only made Zach feel strangely weak and, he hated admitting, rather cowardly.

He gave TJ a narrow-eyed glance. Why would he be afraid to tell her anything? She certainly wasn't an ogre, quite the contrary.

Dammit, in that pink outfit she looked like a mother-to-be, not the owner of a construction company! Her hair was drawn back again, but it was in one of those French braids. And it was the prettiest color, kind of streaked, all sunshine and taffy.

Facing front again, Zach decided he must be getting soft in the head. TJ Reese was not his responsibility. Hell, he hadn't even known her until yesterday.

She was rattling on, explaining the two phases of the company's largest project. Zach only half listened beyond the pleasant sound of her voice. TJ must have been in that accident with Tommy, which was one more horrible aspect of the whole horrible thing.

How did she smile at all? She was a brave little thing, wasn't she?

"Here we are," TJ announced as she pulled the car off the road and into one of the construction areas Zach had driven past last evening. Switching off the ignition, she smiled at her companion. "By the way, I didn't show you your office this morning. It's only a small room, but it will give you a place to hang your hard hat."

"Thanks, TJ," he said softly, still emotionally involved in her unhappy background. "Did I say yesterday that you wouldn't be sorry you hired me?"

"I think you did."

With great tenderness, Zach raised a hand and brushed a golden wisp of hair back from her smooth cheek. "I meant it."

A thrill of alarming magnitude rocketed through TJ's body. The moment was so unexpected she couldn't immediately speak, and she stared into Zach Torelli's amazingly blue eyes until he smiled and reached for the door handle.

Drawing an oddly labored breath, TJ opened her own door. Normal pregnant women didn't get breathless over a virtual stranger's touch, did they? So, did that incredible thrill and a problem with her respiratory system indicate some kind of abnormality?

"There are..." Clearing her throat, TJ began again. "There are hard hats in the trunk." How busily efficient she became opening the trunk! She was embarrassed and not a very accomplished actress. Her cheeks were hot, which was impossible to hide, and she felt almost tongue-tied. But even if her tongue had been free to wag at both ends, what did one say to a man who couldn't possibly have intended what he'd caused?

There had to be something wrong with her. Maybe her hormones were confused. Yes, that was it. When, in heaven's name, had she ever felt something like that shocking thrill with any man? And this outrageously handsome man certainly wasn't personally interested in an eight-months-along pregnant woman!

TJ's longtime habits went into action. Wearing the hard hat, exhibiting complete professionalism, she introduced Zach to the men working on the job. Very quickly he became involved in blueprints and exactly where this particular job was in terms of specific phases of the construction process. What's more, he talked to the men in a way TJ liked, with just enough authority and without patronization.

It was becoming exceedingly apparent that she was one fortunate woman. With Zach supervising the actual construction, her load would be lightened tenfold.

As for her own silly femaleness, she would be better prepared the next time he touched her—if he ever did.

Three

——

With Las Vegas's speeding economy, there were always new developments to work up bids for. Bidding was the rule of the game in the construction business. Some developers handled the entire process themselves, but many wanted a company like TJ's to give them a fixed price of construction and a guaranteed completion date. TJ usually did the initial work on newly offered projects, determining through her own methods whether Reese Home Builders wanted to spend the time and money on the detailed cost study needed to put out a serious bid.

It all boiled down to profit, and she was very good at estimating possible profits from blueprints alone. The project she was presently working on was forty houses in the first phase of a brand-new development, with construction to begin in six weeks. That first phase included four model homes, to be completed within a short deadline, from which the developer would sell unfinished dwellings. It was standard practice in a seller's market, which Vegas had been enjoying for several years.

Engrossed in the work, TJ didn't notice Doreen coming in. The woman cleared her throat, an obvious interruption in the quiet of the office. TJ looked up from her desk. "Oh, hi."

Folding her arms across her chest, Doreen raised an eyebrow. "All right, give. *Where* did you find Torelli?"

When TJ had returned to the office, everything had been rush, rush, rush. Doreen had been juggling phone calls and paperwork, and apparently she had just now found the time to come in and discuss the new super.

TJ put her pen down and raised her arms over her head in a relieving stretch. Sitting for long periods caused that dull ache in the small of her back she'd been noticing more and more of late.

"I didn't find him, he found me," she grinned, not above teasing Doreen a little.

"He just walked in off the street," Doreen remarked in a flatly disbelieving tone while crossing the office to the same chair Zach had occupied earlier.

TJ relented. "He saw my ad and came by last night. I was getting ready to leave when he walked in."

"So, based on his less than one day on the job, what do you think? Or is it too soon for an opinion?"

Arching an eyebrow, TJ smiled again. "Let's hear your opinion first."

Doreen grinned impishly. "He's gorgeous."

"Which will certainly make him a good super, right?" TJ drawled dryly.

Doreen's grin just got bigger. "I know he's qualified for the job or you wouldn't have hired him. But...is he married?"

TJ laughed, then made a face at her secretary. "No, he's not married." Her expression sobered. "Doesn't his name ring a bell?"

"Should it?"

"It was in the newspapers for weeks on end a few months back."

"Torelli . . . Torelli," Doreen intoned thoughtfully. Then her eyes widened. "Vista Construction Company! He's *that* Torelli, the one who went to jail for embezzlement?"

"Good grief, no! Zach *owned* the company. It was his cousin who did all the dirty work. I think they threw away the key on Vincent Torelli. He defrauded several banks and the IRS, bad hombres to steal from. Anyway, Vista went down and Zach needed a job. He read my ad and the rest is history." TJ saw Doreen's worried expression. "What's wrong?"

"Zach was cleared of any complicity, wasn't he?"

"Zach was a victim, pure and simple. He trusted his cousin to manage his money and good old Vincent threw it away in the casinos."

"Hmm."

"You're not convinced."

"Apparently *you* trust him."

"I have no reason not to trust him. You don't, either, Doreen. Look, the man has more talent in his little finger than any other supervisor this company has ever employed had in his entire body."

"Speaking of bodies, Torelli's is definitely worthy of notice," Doreen drawled.

TJ's cheeks got pink. "His looks had nothing to do with giving him the job, and they won't stop me from firing him if he doesn't work out."

Silent a moment, Doreen then got to her feet with a sigh. "I know that. I'm glad you found someone, but I can't help thinking about how many lemons this poor company has tried and tossed out in the past year. What about you? How are you feeling?"

"Much better than I did yesterday at this time. I think Zach *is* going to work out. He's a take-hold kind of man, Doreen."

Doreen nodded. "Well, he's not hanging around the office, anyway." The telephone began ringing. "I'll catch that at my own desk. Talk to you later."

Watching Doreen dashing away, TJ felt a frown developing. Zach's good looks had not influenced her decision to hire him yesterday, but were they influencing her today? If he hadn't touched her hair and cheek...*why* had he touched her? And why did she still feel the intensity of his blue eyes at that moment?

They had visited the other job sites, then returned to the office. Zach had come in only long enough to take a quick look at his designated quarters and to pick up a cellular telephone. She could call him whenever she needed contact, and he wouldn't have to run around looking for a telephone to talk to subcontractors or the office. Cellular phones saved time, and time was money in the construction business.

It was going to work out, Zach was going to work out. She was extremely fortunate to have him on the job, and she wasn't going to start second-guessing the court's opinion that Zach Torelli had been only an innocent bystander, if a terribly injured one, in his cousin's criminal activities.

Construction crews began at six in the morning and stopped working at two, an attempt to elude the afternoon heat. Some subcontractors worked past two, however, independents who were racking up big bucks by covering as many projects as they could squeeze into a day.

Zach traveled from site to site, making sure each one was secure after everyone had finally gone. It was after five when he got into his Wagoneer and headed for the office. He felt great, a little tired, but emotionally pumped up from putting in a good day's work.

And, strange as it seemed, he was anxious to see TJ. There were matters to discuss, a few things he'd spotted that weren't altogether in her favor, places where he could save money. But there was more to the feeling than reasons to talk about the business.

Maybe it was only compassion, he debated uneasily, his mood flipping. Any man with a shred of decency would feel protective about a woman in TJ's situation. A baby coming in a month, a demanding business to run, no husband to help out and memories of tragedy. Poor little gal.

Not that TJ appeared to want sympathy. She seemed to be a strong, calm woman—most of the time. That moment when he'd touched her hair—a regrettable impulse—had shaken her. But then, she hadn't expected it, had she?

Well, neither had he. And it only made good sense to guard against such impulses in the future.

Parking between TJ's Mercedes and a gray Buick, Zach got out of his Wagoneer and went into the building. Its cool, quiet interior felt good, and he went directly to the open door of TJ's office. She was standing at the window, and she turned and saw him.

"Hi," he said with a smile.

"Hi. How'd it go this afternoon?"

Her hopeful expression went right through Zach. It was more important to her that he managed the job well than it was to him, he realized. And that was saying a lot, because he needed this job in the worst way.

But that list of items he'd mentally compiled to discuss with TJ suddenly seemed trivial. He knew what had to be done with each and every one of them, and what good would come out of laying them on her?

No, there was really only one episode of the afternoon that needed discussion. "Mind if I come in for a few minutes?"

"Of course not. Feel free to come to me anytime, Zach."

"Thanks." He approached her desk, but remained standing because she did. "You've got some good men, but I warned two of them about drinking beer on the job this afternoon."

"Cully Mills and Joe Corcoran," TJ said with a sigh. "I've warned them, too."

"Right, Cully and Joe."

"They're extremely competent finish carpenters."

"So I noticed. I don't like drinking on the job, TJ, but I'll adhere to your policy."

She met Zach's steady gaze. There was something in his eyes that made her quickly break the contact. Something personal. Or was her imagination getting ridiculously carried away? Why was she reacting so foolishly to this man?

"Like I said, I warned Joe and Cully, myself. Do whatever you think best, Zach. You're in charge."

He nodded. "Good. I didn't want to overstep my authority, but beer cans strewn all over the project and two carpenters talking silly because they're half-drunk irritates the heck out of me. It's not safe, either."

"I agree."

"Fine. If I have to I'll give them one more warning. But then they're gone, TJ."

TJ's nod contained complete approval, and once again Zach picked up a sense of how relieved she was that he was in control. How, in God's name, had she held the place together without a conscientious superintendent? Running around from project to project in the heat must have drained her.

She reached him. He didn't know whether it was chemistry or hormones, but something in TJ Reese connected with something in him. Was it normal for a man to feel desire for a pregnant woman?

His embarrassment was unfamiliar and unnerving, and TJ would be appalled if she could suddenly read his mind. Clearing his throat, he returned to business. "Do you want me to come by the office in the morning?"

"Only if you feel you need to."

Zach shaped a smile. "I don't plan on spending much time in here, although it's a darned nice office." He indicated the cellular phone attached to his belt. "What about this?"

"Keep it with you. It's been assigned to you, and there's no point in dropping it off at night and having to pick it up again in the morning."

TJ reached for some papers on her desk. "Jim gave me these for you. One's for the IRS and the other one's an application for our group insurance plan."

"All right." Zach came closer to take the papers from her hand, and he accomplished the exchange without a direct look into TJ's eyes. He was beginning to feel like a damned kid with her, and he didn't much like it. He was thirty-six years old, which should be far enough away from boyish awkwardness to find it completely absent from his system.

"So," TJ began briskly, denying herself the extra breath of air she suddenly seemed to need. "Everything went all right this afternoon?"

"I'd say so." The papers were being folded and then refolded. "I'd like to ask you something, TJ. Tell me it's none of my business, if you want to, but do you have any family in Vegas?"

He was worried about her. She could hardly believe it, but this man, whom she'd hired only yesterday and who couldn't possibly know her, was worried about her. "I have very little family," she said softly, profoundly touched that an acquaintance of one day had the ability, and the good sense, to convey concern without pity. "An elderly aunt and uncle in California."

Zach's eyes narrowed on hers. "No parents? No sisters or brothers?"

"I'm afraid not."

"What about in-laws?"

TJ sighed. "A mother-in-law in Florida, but we were never close. Zach, I'm fine. I appreciate your concern, but it's not at all necessary."

He tried to laugh. "Well, family's not always that great, anyway, is it?"

"Not always," TJ agreed, understanding that he was referring to his cousin. "But I'll bet you're from a large family."

Zach shook his head. "It was just me and my cousin for quite a few years, and now...well, I guess that's over, too." He looked at her, inwardly melting at her fragile femininity. How could she be so strong and brave? No family, pregnant, alone...how was she dealing with it all? "Have you picked out names for the baby?" he inquired in the gentlest tone possible.

It was that tone that brought TJ back to reality. She was getting entirely too familiar with a man that she prayed would last but wouldn't be proved dependable for some weeks. Everyone put their best foot forward on the first day of a new job. So far, she was genuinely impressed with Zach Torelli's abilities. But it took time to really know an employee.

"No names yet," TJ lied, and opened her desk drawer for her purse. "Time to go home," she announced in her best telephone voice, the one that told callers all they needed to know about the bright, all-together lady to whom they were speaking.

Zach got the message loud and clear. He'd done it again, crossed that invisible line than most employers drew between themselves and their employees. He'd done the same thing, himself, as Vista's owner. Some employees turned out to be blatant pains in the neck, and until that fact was established or disproved, every experienced employer knew it was best to let friendliness go only so far.

That's all TJ was doing now, trying to keep things businesslike, an attitude he couldn't fault. The fact that she wasn't like any other employer he'd ever known was immaterial. Impending motherhood wasn't a unique condition, just remarkable in her case. Adopting the same withdrawn, remote expression TJ was wearing, Zach followed her into the foyer.

"I'm going to talk to Jim before I leave," TJ said, eliminating a walk together to their cars.

"Fine. See you tomorrow." Touching his forehead in a rather formal salute, Zach turned and exited the building.

TJ had gone the other direction, but when the front door closed, she stopped and leaned against the corridor wall. Gnawing her upper lip, she tried to make sense out of the past few minutes.

"TJ?" Jim was standing in his office doorway, looking apprehensive. "Are you all right?"

"I'm..." She almost said "confused," but admitting confusion wouldn't solve anything. "Going home."

Jim grinned. "The door's in *that* direction."

"So it is." With a tired smile, TJ reversed herself and headed for the outside door. "Bye, Jim. See you tomorrow," she called back to the accountant.

"Drive carefully," he returned.

TJ did drive carefully, but out of habit, not concentration. She couldn't make heads or tails of her weird feelings around Zach Torelli, and that confused hormone theory seemed utterly ludicrous. It was her brain that was confused, not her stupid hormones! What in heck was wrong with her? She was eight months pregnant and acting like a virginal fourteen-year-old with a bad crush on some poor, unsuspecting boy!

And what was going on with Torelli? Did the man think she had only barely survived until he'd come along? If that was the case, he had an ego problem.

Home was a pretty, white stucco house with a red tile roof, and TJ was glad to get there. Inside, the first thing she did was kick off her shoes. Then, sprawled on her living room sofa, she stared at the ceiling. Granted, Jim and Doreen were concerned about her, too. Zach certainly didn't have a monopoly on worry about the boss. But Jim and Doreen had a lot more right to worry than Torelli did.

TJ released an exasperated breath. A *right* to worry? Lord, she was slipping off the deep end! Groaning out loud, TJ wrestled her bulky self up and off of the sofa. A long, cool bath was what she needed.

The days passed, with TJ refusing to give in to a silly urge to primp and put on makeup before leaving the house in the morning. Although, she decided, she certainly could use a good haircut. She used to wear her hair in a blunt-cut, shoulder-length bob, and the style had been a lot more becoming than that clasp at the back of her neck, or even the French braid she sometimes arranged.

Actually, she had let herself go much too long without a trip to a beauty parlor. And facing that fact had nothing to do with Zach Torelli, she told herself.

It was a lie, of course, which she knew with far too much certainty. Zach *did* have something to do with suddenly wanting to look nice. Even though looking nice was almost impossible with a forty-inch waist.

Doreen was no help. "I think Zachary likes you," she declared while delivering some letters for TJ's signature one afternoon.

"Well, I certainly hope so," TJ retorted, hoping to throw her nosy secretary off that scent. Whether Zach's "liking" went beyond mere friendship, which was what Doreen was implying, was something TJ had been puzzling enough about without outside interference. "I doubt if he would work very long for someone he *didn't* like."

"Don't play coy, TJ. You know darned well I'm not talking about employer-employee relations." She giggled. "I think Zachary's got relations in mind, but not that kind."

TJ sat back and purposely looked disgusted. "Relations with a pregnant woman? Come on, Doreen, give me a break."

"Listen, sweetie, some men are turned on by pregnancy."

"Where did you pick up that scintillating bit of information?"

"You don't believe me, do you? Well, I can prove it. I'll bring you the book."

"What's its theme, kinky sex?"

Doreen laughed. "It's a textbook, smart-pants."

"Left over from your college days?"

"You know I never throw anything away. Anyway, *you* feel clumsy, but not every man sees you that way."

TJ shook her head. "You were pregnant twice. Did *you* feel attractive at eight months?"

"Lord, no. But I'll tell you something, sweetie, Jack thought I was. The doctor told me to abstain the final month and Jack nearly went crazy."

"Yes, but you and Jack were married and in love." TJ broke off when Doreen broke up. "You're yanking my chain, aren't you?"

"Not really," Doreen said with a final spurt of giggles, plopping into one of the chairs across from TJ's desk. "What I said about that textbook is true. I really will bring it to you."

"Please don't. I'm not interested in psychoanalyzing my self or anyone else."

"I think you're missing the boat. Zachary's not only gorgeous, he understands your line of work. What could be better?"

"A secretary who minds her own business?" TJ queried in a sweetly pointed tone.

Doreen waved a casual hand. "I'm only thinking about your future, boss."

TJ grinned indulgently and turned her attention to the letters awaiting her signature. She felt Doreen's unwavering gaze while she wielded the pen, but didn't realize how serious the usually lighthearted woman had become until the last letter had been signed and TJ had looked up.

"You've had a hard time of it," Doreen said quietly. "But don't let one bad experience ruin every chance you get to know other men."

"Is that what I'm doing?" TJ asked in an equally subdued tone.

Rising, Doreen reached for the completed letters. "I tease and cut up a lot, TJ, but I think you know I'm on your team."

"Yes, I do know that." TJ smiled. "But I think matchmaking is a little premature, don't you? Give me a couple more months, okay?"

Doreen's normal gamine grin appeared. "Will do. But watch out then, sweetie!"

"And don't work on Zach, either," TJ called as Doreen swept out of the room. She was positive Doreen heard her, but the secretary made no response. Shaking her head in amusement, TJ got back to work.

* * *

Zach felt that his job was going well. He had established a good rapport with the company men, and the subcontractors were rapidly learning that he would not accept substandard work. No phase of the construction process escaped his scrutiny. He was working hard and putting in long hours, but he was also sleeping well and awakening eager to face each day.

He had squeezed apartment hunting into his busy schedule, renting one that was in a complex less than a mile from the office, and had given notice to his present landlord. He would make the move at the end of the month, which was another matter settled.

There was only one gray area in his life, his own plans for the future. He wanted TJ to know he wasn't a permanent employee. Not that he wouldn't be in her employ for some time yet. But by his calculations, at his present rate of pay he would have enough cash accumulated to go back into business in less than a year, and he didn't want her counting on a long-term association.

Zach cursed his lack of foresight every time he thought of his initial interview, which was when he should have told TJ about his plans. She probably still would have hired him, but she would be aware of his intentions, which she had every right to know.

By the end of his second week, the matter was driving Zach up the wall. TJ was so obviously pleased with his work, her every smile was like rubbing salt into a raw wound. Her easy compliments pricked his conscience, and the fact that she rarely showed up at any of the job sites to check on his progress was a trust he couldn't keep on accepting, not when he was deliberately misleading her.

He decided it was showdown time. Delaying the inevitable would only make it worse. TJ *had* to know that he wouldn't be around next year.

The opportunity came when she called him on the cell phone and asked him to stop in the office before he went home that afternoon. "I want you to look over the figures Jim and I put together on a new bid, Zach."

She and Jim had bid a lot of jobs in the past without anyone else's input, but TJ was turning to him more and more for advice, Zach realized, frowning about how she might take his confession.

It had to be done, though, a cruel blow to her trust or not. He'd gotten himself into this situation, and only he could clear it up.

He arrived at the office just as Doreen was leaving for the day. She waved and smiled and then stood by while he got out of the Wagoneer. "How's it going, Zachary?"

It amused Zach that Doreen preferred using his given name. "Fine here. How's it going with you?"

"Can't complain. I understand you're moving to this side of town."

"At the end of the month."

"Great! If you need any help, let me know. Jack and I are good movers."

"Thanks, but all I'll be moving are clothes and a few personal possessions."

"Oh, you're renting furnished."

Zach avoided self-pity like the plague, but there were moments when a memory would give him a jolt. He used to live in a beautiful, custom-built home, and it was quite a drop in life-style from that to a furnished apartment.

He conquered the memory with a crooked smile. "Thanks for the offer. TJ's expecting me. See you on Monday." Strolling to the front door, he heard Doreen call out, "You'll have to come to dinner sometime. I'd like you to meet Jack and the kids."

"Thanks." Shooting Doreen a smile of acceptance, he went on in.

TJ was coming down the corridor, probably from Jim's office, and her slow, almost cautious movements tore at Zach's heartstrings. Her body had broadened considerably during the past two weeks, and the color of her eyes seemed oddly paler than it had been, her bosom fuller, her skin creamier. She was in the final stage of her pregnancy, getting very close to the birth of her baby, and her appearance was both ripe and fragile, an inconsistency he had never noticed in any other woman.

His gaze flicked downward and past the hem of her skirt. However broad her beam, TJ had great legs, a pretty curving of calves to slender ankles that appealed to the maleness in him.

Today she was wearing a mint green sleeveless dress with a pleated front, and after taking it in, Zach saw what was really different about her. She'd changed her hairstyle. It was floating around her face, kissing her shoulders, softening her features.

"I like your hair," he said, and was rewarded with a faint pinkish stain in each of her cheeks.

"Thank you." TJ walked past him, catching his scent of dust, sweat and after-shave. "Come into my office. I've got the bid proposal I want you to see on my desk."

"I'm dirty." He was. A hot wind blowing for most of the day had turned the dry desert soil of the construction sites into dust bowls.

She smiled. "A little desert dust won't hurt this place. Sit down."

He complied, but slowly. A vein pulsed in his jaw. Before they started talking business, he was going to explain his future plans. And, heaven help him, he didn't want to hurt TJ. He didn't want to see disappointment in her eyes, nor the effects of a blow she didn't deserve.

He held on to one small reserve of hopefulness: Maybe she wasn't as dependent on him as she appeared to be. Maybe his own ego was making him feel more important than he really was.

Sitting very straight, he watched her arrange herself in her desk chair. "TJ, before we get to that bid, there's another matter we need to talk about."

She smiled expectantly.

Four

Zach had the floor, and wishing he didn't have to do this was making his stomach knot. "I've been working here almost two weeks."

"Yes?" It was both affirmation and curiosity.

"TJ, this is something I should have told you at our first meeting."

She was beginning to sense something awry, although what it could be escaped her. "Go on, Zach."

He tried to get more comfortable in his chair, which was impossible when he was so tense. "I'll probably only be working for you for six, eight months," he finally blurted.

TJ sat very still, attempting to digest what she'd just heard. "Well, I appreciate your telling me, but may I know your reason? From my standpoint I'm extremely pleased with the relationship. I guess I never stopped to wonder if *you* were content working for me."

"It's not that at all. This is a darned good job, and if all I wanted was a job for the rest of my life, I'd stay here as long as you'd let me." Zach leaned forward, his expression anxious. It was important to him that she understood. "I want my own company again, TJ. I've got dozens of plans and ideas. I'll operate differently than I did with Vista. Everyone knows I put too much trust in one man, but Vincent would never have been able to get away with theft for so long if I'd been more alert. I have to take some of the responsibility for Vista's failure, because I failed, too. I won't fail again."

How fervent he looked and sounded. TJ stared at the man across her desk and felt the fire of his emotions, understanding for the first time how deeply scarred he was by the loss of his company.

"TJ, why did you have such a hard time finding a decent super?"

She blinked, forcing herself to concentrate on Zach's change of subject. "Bad luck, maybe. I really don't know. No one with any real knowledge or scruples came along, I guess." God, she would have to start that dreadful search again. Not for a few more months, thank goodness. And once the baby was born, she would be better able to get around to do whatever needed doing.

But she had been so comfortable with Zach on the job. Two weeks shouldn't have been long enough to form habits, but she knew that she'd been looking forward to a less stressful workload than she'd lived with before. And she did so want the time to get to know her baby.

Actually she felt like bawling. One of those teary sessions was sneaking up on her, which would only embarrass both her and Zach. She cleared her throat. "You have every right to live your life the way you want to. Thank you for giving me so much notice. I'm sure . . ."

"TJ, I'll help you find another super before I leave. I promise."

Oh, oh. Now she really felt like bawling. Sometimes kindness was tougher to deal with than any other human trait. She had to compose herself or look like a complete idiot.

Rising as quickly as her bulk allowed, TJ went to the window and turned her back on Zach. Tears were making her eyes burn, but she managed a relatively normal voice. "We can talk about this again later on, maybe after... September."

Was she crying? The possibility made Zach sick at heart. But her back was stiff with pride, and instinct warned him that she would reject an offer of condolence. "Whatever you say," he said quietly. "I'm sorry I didn't tell you about this during our first meeting."

"Yes, it would have been best," she agreed, finally able to turn around and face him again. "But what's done is done. Let's forget it for now and go over that bid."

Zach stood up. "You're tired. Let me take the information home with me. I'll go over it tonight and we can talk about it tomorrow. Oh. Are you coming in tomorrow?"

"I usually come in on Saturdays, but I was planning on staying home tomorrow." TJ didn't want to go into detail with Zach, but her feet felt swollen and she had been looking longingly at a totally free weekend. She was visiting her doctor on every Thursday now. He was cheerful and optimistic about her good health, but she knew that she was tiring more easily and feeling dragged out by the end of each day.

"Don't change your plans. We can talk on the phone. I'll be working, but you can reach me on the cellular."

"I suppose that would be all right." TJ glanced at the ringing telephone on her desk. "Excuse me," she murmured, picking up the phone. "Reese Home Builders."

Zach walked away, thoroughly upset with himself and the whole situation. TJ needed a husband. *Any* woman in her situation needed a husband. Not a boyfriend, damn it to hell, a *husband!* Today's free and easy attitude on single parenting wasn't for him. And she shouldn't be running herself ragged with this company, either. Not now, and not after the baby came.

He finger-combed his hair in a completely agitated gesture. He shouldn't have told her about his plans. All he'd done was make her feel bad and add another worry to her already overlong list of worries.

She was really getting to him, wasn't she? This pretty little woman with her tired gray green eyes and brave smile? Sure, she could talk construction. Better, probably, than any man he knew. TJ understood the business inside and out. You couldn't trip her up on construction terms, methods, tools of the trade or just plain savvy.

But she was still a woman. Women fought as hard as men did for a decent living, but women had the babies and cried over disappointments. What man could do any better job than she was doing? And she was nearly nine months pregnant!

Sometimes life was too damned hard!

Zach knew his expression was grim. Any man could count himself lucky to have TJ for a wife. *Any* man, himself included.

The thought nearly flattened him. TJ was talking on the phone, obviously a business conversation, and Zach stared at her with a thundering heartbeat. Him and TJ, married? Would she fall down laughing if he hinted at any such liaison?

Hell, yes, she would, or else she would show him the door, superintendent or not!

Besides, when had the idea of marriage become appealing? Ever since he'd been old enough to enjoy the facts of life, he'd avoided matrimony.

But then, he'd never met a woman quite like TJ, either, had he?

Zach shook his head in utter amazement. He didn't even know what "TJ" stood for. In fact, he knew very little about his lady boss. Certainly little beyond this office. Where was her home? Who were her friends? How did she live? Casually? Formally? Alone? With a housekeeper or companion?

She was so darned vulnerable, and the funny thing was, he wasn't sure she even knew it.

TJ put down the phone. Zach had been giving her such peculiar looks, and she wasn't sure what to make of them. His information about leaving the company after six or eight months was like a lead weight in her midsection, but what could she do about it? His reason was sound, even admirable, and he would be here during her most trying months.

"Let's call it a day," she said quietly, picking up the bid documents and tucking them into a file folder. "I'll be home all day tomorrow. Call me whenever it's convenient for you." TJ scribbled on the front of the folder. "This is my home number."

Zach returned to the desk and accepted the folder. His eyes were dark and somber. "I wish I could do more to help you."

Her gaze jumped to his. So many times she had caught that note of protectiveness in Zach's voice, and she had consistently tried to overlook it. But there was no pretending it didn't exist at this moment. His eyes contained compassion and affection, and he was looking at her as though she were a responsibility shirked. "You're doing your job. What more should you do?"

"Anything that might need doing. I mean it, TJ. If there's anything..."

"Please," she interjected, stopping him for her own comfort. His kindness was making her feel helpless, and she wasn't helpless. Granted, she was entering a period of time when having a strong, loving man to lean on would be wonderful. But she didn't, and while this was all new and apparently disturbing to Zach, she had lived with its reality for nearly nine months.

They walked out together, TJ carrying her purse, Zach carrying the file folder. He escorted her to her car and opened the door for her.

Stopping abruptly, TJ held up a finger. "Oh, I just remembered something. Would you check with the carpenters and find out if one of them would come over to my house on Sunday? I meant to take care of that myself today, but..."

"To do what?"

"Install some shelving in the nursery."

"I'll do it."

TJ tensed. "Zach . . ."

"I'll do it, TJ. I *want* to do it."

They began a stare-down, which TJ ultimately lost. What difference did it make who did the work? And Zach seemed so determined to help. "All right, thanks."

Zach held out the file folder and the gold pen from his shirt pocket. "Write down your address."

It was accomplished quickly. Passing back the folder and pen, TJ got behind the wheel. Zach bent down to see into the car. "Any particular time on Sunday?"

TJ gave her head a negative shake. "Whenever's convenient for you."

"What about materials?"

"I have the shelves and brackets at the house."

"All right. Look for me around three."

With another "Thanks," TJ started her car. Zach closed the door and stood by while she backed out of the parking space. As she drove away, she glanced into the rearview mirror and saw him watching. Just standing there and watching. It gave her a funny feeling, a slipping and sliding of emotions that was pure female and not altogether pleasant.

In fact, the sensation was much more disturbing than pleasant, although if she wasn't so obviously pregnant and ungainly . . .

TJ's eyes narrowed. Why would a man with Zachary Torelli's appeal appear to be interested in a woman in her situation? Because she was the boss? Some people couldn't help buttering up the boss, a distasteful trait. If that's all Zach's attentions meant, though, wouldn't she sense it?

She simply did not know how to interpret the subleties of Zach's tones and expressions. Chalk it up to inexperience, TJ thought wryly. It had been an awfully long time since she'd had a reason to debate a man's intentions.

Tommy had turned out to be such a rounder, although in the early years of their marriage, they had been happy. They had both worked hard getting the company started, and those long, exhausting days had been their best. Once the pressure had eased up and they were making money, Tommy had changed. It had been painful to face, but TJ had gradually had to accept that she wasn't enough for her big, handsome, sexy husband. No one woman was enough.

Poor Tommy. That's how TJ thought of him now, which seemed so sad to her. Why would anyone, man or woman, exchange the good things of life, which certainly had been hers and Tommy's for the taking, for meaningless pleasure? At least, TJ assumed Tommy had derived pleasure from his women and drinking.

Who really knew? she thought with a long sigh.

At any rate, other than Tommy, her experience with men would never make a novel. Which certainly didn't give her any degree of expertise on figuring out Zachary Torelli.

Or, maybe more importantly, herself.

That evening Zach studied the bid sheets TJ had given him. He called her on Saturday morning and made a couple of suggestions, which they discussed in a businesslike manner. With a reminder that he would be by her house around three the next afternoon to install that shelving, he said goodbye and broke the connection.

Dinner was a solitary affair in a crowded restaurant, and then, feeling restless, Zach drove down the Strip. It was a mistake in judgment. The Strip, with its millions of neon bulbs in garish designs and colors advertising its dozens of casinos, was bumper-to-bumper traffic. Saturday night was not the best time for a casual drive on the Strip, which every Las Vegas resident knew and most avoided.

Making a right turn at Twain Street, Zach escaped the bright lights and headed east. A few more turns and he was on Desert Inn Road, still moving east. But this section of the city was miles north of TJ's office building and her home, and Zach worked his route south and east. He was driving with the air conditioner off and the windows open. The night air was fabulous, cool and silky on his skin. Daytime temperatures were still reaching ninety-four, ninety-five degrees, but the nights were cooling down now, a great time of the year.

He finally reached the office building and drove past it slowly. Night lights illuminated several windows and the parking lot, but the place was silent and deserted.

He had memorized TJ's home address but told himself he was only taking a drive, not deliberately looking for her house. Then he had to stop kidding himself, because there it was right in front of him.

"Nice," he murmured, taking in the shrubs, trees and neatly trimmed lawn around the white stucco structure.

He headed back across town then, wondering just what it was that was making him behave so uncharacteristically. He didn't have to spend Saturday nights alone. There were people he could have called, men friends, women friends.

But one small pregnant lady was taking up his thoughts. Why? Merely because of that vulnerability he kept picking up from TJ? Or was there more to the throbbing discontent in his body than a desire to help a fellow human being?

There was a *lot* more to it, Zach had to admit, albeit grimly. His feelings for TJ might be confusing, but they were too insistent to be ignored. How would she take hearing that he had advanced beyond ordinary affection for her? The memory of that startling thought about marriage still knocked him for a loop whenever it popped into his mind, which it seemed to be doing with unnerving regularity. In the first place, TJ would think he was pretty weird if he started talking about marriage between the two of them, and in the second, why in hell would he want to get married?

It was TJ making him think such crazy things, her and her pretty gray green eyes and sweet personality. Oh, yes, when she wasn't talking business, she was as sweetly feminine as any woman could be. And even during a business discussion Zach could see beneath TJ's pragmatic expressions to the softer, gentler woman.

Besides that, though, there was something about her carrying a child, something about the miracle of birth and motherhood, about *knowing* that a tiny person was in her body...

Zach slowly shook his head. He was behaving as though he'd never known a pregnant woman before. He was going through the strangest conglomeration of emotions he'd ever come up against, and just how was a man supposed to deal with something he didn't begin to understand?

He slept fitfully that night, awakening in the morning with an odd elation. Today he was going to TJ's house. He was going to see how she lived, and if this wasn't an opportunity to get to know her better, what would be?

The house never got really dirty anymore, TJ thought as she walked around with a dust cloth. Neat by nature, she always picked up after herself, which kept everything in its place. Once-a-week vacuuming and dusting was about all she needed to do in spare moments, and about once a month a cleaning service came in and did the tiled floors, the windows and any other major chore she might name.

The yard and swimming pool were another matter. She had regular yard and pool maintenance, which was more of a necessity than a luxury. No way could she push a lawn mower, and cleaning the pool simply took too much time.

With the house immaculate and herself bathed and dressed in a favorite at-home garment, a colorful, ankle-length caftan, TJ awaited three o'clock. She had done very little entertaining since Tommy's death, and Zach coming by to put up shelving could hardly be construed as a social engagement.

But it felt like one. An excitement she wasn't altogether comfortable with made even her skin tingle. After a day and a half at home, TJ was alert and bright eyed. She had read, slept and simply relaxed, and was very satisfied with her weekend off.

Behind all those quiet hours, though, had been that lurking excitement. She felt like a woman waiting for a man. If she was slim, she would have worn something much prettier. As it was, she felt larger than she was, heavy-footed and ungraceful, and glossy flowing hair and even a little makeup couldn't atone for ungainliness.

Her confinement would soon be over, though, and the thought of holding her baby, of caring for it, loving it, made up for any and all discomforts she had to accept now.

The front doorbell rang at five minutes to three. TJ opened the door with a smile and a fluttering heartbeat. "I do like prompt people," she declared. "Come in."

Zach gave her long dress an approving glance. He was wearing faded, comfortable jeans and a white polo shirt. In place of the cowboy boots he preferred on workdays was a pair of sneakers. He carried a small toolbox. "You look rested," he commented.

"I feel rested." TJ led the way into her living room. "Can I get you something? A soft drink, iced tea, a beer?"

Zach grinned. "I'll take you up on that offer when the shelves are up, okay?"

"Of course. This way." Gesturing to another doorway, TJ then preceded Zach to the bedroom she had turned into a nursery. Directly across the hall from the master suite, the room was painted a pale yellow and contained a crib and all sorts of infant paraphernalia.

Everything about the room and its furnishings touched Zach, and he took his time looking around. "Very nice," he said softly.

"Yes, it is, isn't it?" TJ agreed. "It's been ready for months now. I just realized recently that a few shelves would be helpful." She walked over to one wall. "I'd like them installed here."

"Fine. Where are they?"

"In the garage. I'll show you."

They traipsed through the house again and used the connecting door between the kitchen and garage. There were two prefinished four-foot shelves and brackets to carry in, which Zach easily toted back to the nursery. TJ showed him exactly where she wanted the shelves, and he got to work.

"I like your house," Zach remarked, busy with a measuring tape and straightedge.

TJ sat down in the rocking chair she had bought especially for this room. "Thanks."

"What's its size?"

"Twenty-one hundred square feet."

"Three bedrooms?"

"Yes." His back was to the room, and TJ had an unrestricted view of his muscular shoulders and quite notable behind. Taut, masculine buns in faded denim was an arousing sight for any healthy female, and TJ looked because she couldn't seem to stop herself. But there was a lot more to admire in this man than a great physique. He was kind, and Tommy hadn't been. Even in the beginning, Tommy hadn't been as kind as Zach.

"And you live here alone?"

"Only for another couple weeks," TJ replied solemnly, drawing an amused over-the-shoulder glance from Zach. She smiled.

"Right." He grinned and turned back to the wall.

TJ rocked back and forth. It was very pleasant to sit there and watch Zach work. He knew exactly what he was doing, but so did TJ, and she understood the economy and efficiency of Zach's methods. This was a job she could have done herself if the shelves hadn't been so heavy. According to her doctor, she could do anything she was accustomed to doing, except for lifting.

"Did the company build this house?" Zach asked, standing back to eyeball his measurements.

"No, we...I'm its second owner." That "we" meant her and Tommy, and Zach felt the sorrow of her situation again. "I've lived here about three years now," TJ added. "It's a quiet neighborhood, which I like."

"Mostly adults?"

"There are some children."

Zach sent her a warm glance. "And soon to be one more."

Smiling, TJ laid her hand on her tummy. "Were you ever married?"

"Never found the right woman."

"Then I guess I won't ask about children."

Zach laughed. "No children, TJ."

"But you like children. I don't really know why I feel that from you, but I do."

"I haven't been around kids very much. How about you?"

Surprised by the question, TJ frowned slightly. "I guess I haven't been, either, which I never really thought about before. I see Doreen's kids once in a while, but not often enough to get close to them. It's like that with the children of other people I know, too. Hmm."

"Hmm, what? You're not worried about being a good mother, are you? You shouldn't be. You'll be a terrific mother."

He was facing her, standing some distance away, but looking at her with those incredible blue eyes and touching her soul in some unfathomable way. "I'd like to have children," he said softly.

"Then I'm sure you will."

She had stopped rocking and he had stopped working, and there was more being said between them than the words coming out of their mouths. TJ sat there and allowed it to happen for several long moments. Such rapport was unusual and maybe something special. Her breathing was shallow, barely discernible. He was a beautiful man—both physically and emotionally—and she had never connected so solidly with anyone before in her life.

Then, finally, he broke the almost hypnotic spell with a smile. "What does 'TJ' stand for?"

She tired to swallow and realized how dry her mouth had become. "Teresa Jane. My dad tagged me 'TJ' before I could walk and it's been 'TJ' ever since. Let me get us both something to drink." Rising from the rocker, TJ hurried from the room.

In the kitchen she gratefully sucked on an ice cube while she prepared two glasses of lemonade. It seemed almost insane to imagine herself falling for Zach Torelli, but her body was acting very strangely. Apparently pregnancy didn't stifle a woman's emotions, or maybe it was that very condition *making* her behave so irrationally.

But what was Zach's excuse? There was nothing wrong with *his* hormones! And he kept telling her that she was an attractive, desirable woman—by expression, by innuendo, by tone of voice, in every way possible, if one wanted to get down to brass tacks. Why would he do that when she *wasn't* attractive, and as far as desirable went, how on earth could a man who hadn't caused it find this figure stimulating?

TJ carried the two glasses back to the nursery and handed one to Zach. "If you don't have other plans, maybe you'd like to stay for dinner," she said quietly, making it an invitation he could easily refuse.

He took a big swallow of his lemonade. "Even if I'd arrived with other plans I'd cancel them. Thank you, I'd like to stay for dinner."

"In that case, I'll go see what's on hand."

"Don't go to any trouble. Anything will be fine with me."

There was that innate kindness again. The man had the ability to take her breath away with a few lovely words. How, in heaven's name, had he stayed single for so long? If he was this nice to every woman he met...

But maybe he wasn't. Maybe she had something he wanted.

"You go ahead and finish this while I see what's in the refrigerator," she said through suddenly benumbed lips. She certainly didn't have a svelte, sexy body, but she did have one thing Zachary might want, a successful construction business.

The thought was horrifying, and on the return trip to the kitchen TJ tried to destroy it, to shatter it into minute, irreparable pieces. She didn't want it in her mind, and she wished it had never occured to her. What was the basis for such harsh suspicion, his admission about wanting his own company again? Surely if he was inclined to do something so devious, he wouldn't have told her his future plans, would he?

TJ leaned against a kitchen counter, her legs weak and unsteady. What should she think? The only man she'd ever been close to—Tommy—had deceived her for a long time before she finally woke up. Even at that it had taken another length of time for her to accept, to really believe Tommy's infidelity. And in the end, she had still fought reality, *still* attempted one more reconciliation.

Well, that she would never regret. Without that one night of lovemaking, she wouldn't be having a child in two more weeks. TJ wrapped her arms around her bulging waist, as if to protect the life within it. There was nothing more important than her baby, nothing.

But it would be very nearsighted to minimize the importance of financial security, which Reese Home Builders gave her. She was self-supporting because of that company, and only a complete fool would risk her economic future.

She wasn't a fool, not when it came to her child's welfare. If Zach had any such notions about her...?

TJ groaned. She was condemning a man because he was kind and thoughtful, and because she was worried about some admiring looks. How could she? Where was her usual sense of fair play?

Chagrined, TJ moved to the refrigerator and yanked it open.

And then, standing there with her hand on the refrigerator door, she experienced a shooting pain in her lower abdomen. It was there and gone so fast she wasn't sure what had happened. Frowning, she closed the fridge and went to a chair and sat down. She felt strange, she realized, a trifle breathless, slightly light-headed.

TJ placed her hands on her distended abdomen and sat there for several minutes. Nothing happened, no more weird pains, no sudden enlightenment of what that one had meant.

Fine. She would see to dinner. From the bedroom area of the house she could hear Zach, and she was the one who had instigated dinner plans. Rising, TJ returned to the refrigerator.

Ten minutes later she was tearing lettuce for a salad when another pain struck. This one took her breath and lasted for several seconds. Leaning against the counter, her eyes widened in understanding. It was happening a few weeks early, but she was going into labor.

Everything was ready for the hospital. An overnight case packed with essentials had been prepared weeks ago. She would wait a little longer to make sure before she called her doctor, but she knew. Deep inside, she knew. A soft smile curved her lips. Her baby was coming ... today.

Five

——

Zach strolled into the kitchen. "The shelves are up. Want to take a look?" TJ was sitting on a chair next to the table. The tiled sink counter contained a teak bowl and an array of salad vegetables. The tinted window in the oven door radiated light and warmth, and Zach could see a casserole within. He took everything in quickly and brought his gaze back to TJ. Something was in the air, a feeling, intangible but indisputably there. "Are you all right?"

"I'm..." TJ had almost said that she was fine, a purely automatic response. "It's the baby. Things are beginning to happen."

A spear of electricity seemed to bolt through Zach's system. "Now? Right this minute?"

The man had actually paled, which struck TJ as funny. This big, strong man was blanching at the mere thought of childbirth. Her laugh was cut short by another pain. "Oh, that was a good one," she breathed when it was over. Zach's whole body was twitching, as if he wanted to do something and just didn't know what. "It's not going to happen right this minute," TJ soothed. "Don't be alarmed."

"But, TJ... shouldn't we—*you*—be doing something?"

"I've called my doctor. Everything's under control."

He raked his hair and took a long breath. "I'll drive you to the hospital."

TJ nodded. "Thanks, I'd appreciate a ride. I was going to call a neighbor or a taxi, but..."

"Are you bringing anything with you?" Zach's gaze jumped around the kitchen. "I'll put this food away."

He was as nervous as a cat, gathering up lettuce and tomatoes and celery and stuffing them into the refrigerator crisper drawer. TJ felt quite calm herself, and found Zach's agitation humorous if endearing. She could never have envisioned having a man around at this particular moment. For months, she'd planned procedure. It was a matter of organization, she'd figured. Her suitcase was ready, and there were several neighbors who had said they would be more than happy to drive her to the hospital when the time came. If no one was available, there was always a taxi.

Zach being here was a piece of luck, but he was behaving as though he'd lost his sense of direction. TJ tried not to laugh again, but the way he was dashing back and forth between the refrigerator and the counter was pretty funny.

Maintaining a straight face, she got to her feet. "I'll..."

Zach whirled. "What are you doing?"

"I was just..." Surprised by the strong hands on her shoulders, she allowed Zach to steer her back down to the chair. "Zach, really, I'm fine. I was only going to turn off the oven and take out the casserole."

"I'll do it. You tell me what you want done and I'll do it! And let's hurry!"

He was in much worse condition than she was, TJ realized. This was new to her, too, although she wasn't frightened by it. But then, the inevitability of childbirth was so vividly manifest to her, and it might not be to Zach. Still, her pains were ten minutes apart, and there was plenty of time to do the few things necessary for her to leave the house with a clear mind.

But rather than argue with a distraught man, she would allow him to take charge. That's what Zach seemed to want, and it did feel good to have someone with her right now. "All right," TJ smiled. "Turn off the oven and put the casserole in the refrigerator."

Zach wondered if TJ was seeing a quivering mass of jelly when she looked at him. That's what he felt like inside, all oozy and disoriented. He'd never experienced anything quite like it before. He was shaken, worried and scared spitless. He wanted everything quickly taken care of so they could head for the hospital. Switching the oven dial to Off, he took care of the casserole.

He glanced around. The food was put away and the kitchen in comparatively good order. "What else?" he questioned anxiously.

"There's a small blue suitcase in the closet in my bedroom. It's all ready to go. Here, take these and put them in the right-hand drawer of the smallest bureau." TJ removed a ring and her watch and handed them to Zach.

Zach took off at a gallop, racing through the house to the master bedroom. He stopped in the doorway. The room was decorated in soft grays and mauves, a pleasing, attractive color scheme. His gaze went to the bed, TJ's bed. It had meaning, and Zach drew a sharp, quick breath. He shouldn't be thinking of such things at a time like this, but he could almost see TJ in that bed.

Burying the disturbing image, he went to the bureau and put away TJ's jewelry, then to the closet. It was large and extremely well organized. Gratefully he noted that it contained only female garments. Oddly, now that he thought about it, he'd seen nothing of Tommy anywhere in the house.

Zach came out of the closet with the blue suitcase and looked around the bedroom again. This was the room for photographs, if TJ was so inclined.

There wasn't even a small snapshot tucked into the frame of the mirror, nothing, not the slightest hint that TJ had once shared this room with a husband.

Puzzling about it, Zach hurried back to the kitchen.

TJ was waiting, but she had made two brief telephone calls during Zach's absence, one to Doreen and the other to her closest neighbor. She was ready to leave for the hospital.

Zach paced the waiting room and hospital corridors. What was taking so long? It was nearly eight in the evening, and the nurses just kept telling him that Mrs. Reese was doing fine.

The maternity wing was a busy place. People dashed up and down the halls, doctors, nurses, visitors. Zach had inspected every foot of the public areas, even to standing at the nursery window and staring at the dozens of infants in their tiny beds. He got into a conversation with one of the fathers who'd come to admire his son.

"Which one's yours?" the young man asked.

Zach cleared his throat. "My...lady is still in the...what do you call it?"

"The delivery room?"

"Probably." He was so in the dark, Zach realized, an outsider, not really a part of the activity around him. He studied the young man. "Were you there during your son's birth?"

"Wouldn't have missed it for anything."

Zach wished he could be with TJ, holding her hand if nothing else. She should have someone with her, as this man's wife did.

Zach walked away from the window and the proud father, feeling choked up, more emotional than he could ever remember being. TJ touched him like no one ever had. Their life paths had collided and mingled in the past few weeks, altering his goals, his desires, his very personality. A business of his own was still important, but so was his and TJ's relationship.

Today was a milestone. Once the baby came, TJ might be receptive to a relationship. She was too young to live indefinitely without a man.

Without a lover.

Zach's heart beat faster with the thought. Yes, he'd thought of TJ in that context before. And maybe thinking about it today was out of line. But she wasn't just a boss or a friend to him; she was a woman he wanted. How odd that one particular woman could make every other female unappealing to a man.

This was getting serious, Zach admitted with a deeply concerned frown. Shoving his hands into his jeans pockets, he leaned against the window casing and stared out. It was dark outside, but he wasn't trying to see anywhere but into his own soul, anyway.

"Zachary!"

Turning, Zach saw Doreen and a man walking up. "Hi, Doreen."

"This is my husband, Jack. Honey, this is Zachary Torelli."

The two men shook hands. Zach saw a short, stocky man with dark blond hair and hazel eyes. He was dressed very much as Zach was, in jeans and a casual knit shirt.

"How's TJ?" Doreen asked.

"I don't know a damned thing, other than that she's doing all right," Zach answered with some disgust.

"I called, but that's all I heard, too. I'm going to go and talk to the nurse."

Jack grinned as his wife darted away. "She's on pins and needles, worse than when she was the one having the baby."

"You've been through this twice?"

"A boy and a girl. Do you have any kids?"

"No."

"Doreen thought you might still be here. TJ called this afternoon and said you were going to drive her to the hospital."

"I couldn't just leave her here all alone."

Jack nodded. "I'm sure TJ will apreciate it. She's a nice lady who's had more than her share of problems."

It occurred to Zach that this man probably knew a lot about TJ and Tommy. Their marriage couldn't have been all that great, not when TJ didn't display even one photograph of her husband.

"I feel for her, Jack. She's a square shooter and she got a pretty raw deal."

Jack nodded solemnly. "Yes, she did. But she's a strong woman, Zachary, and the baby will give her a lot of comfort."

Zach hesitated, nearly rebutting Jack's opinion of TJ's strength before he thought about it. It was possible he saw her differently than Jack did, possible, actually, that he saw her differently than *anyone* else did. Zach realized then that he could pump this man for information and probably learn a whole slew of facts about TJ.

Something within him balked at the idea. Whatever he learned about Tommy and TJ, he'd rather hear it from TJ— if she ever trusted him enough to open up.

That's one thing he was going to work on, gaining TJ's personal trust. She already trusted him on a business level, which was gratifying but not nearly enough for him. What he really wanted from TJ was becoming bigger and more complex than anything he'd ever come up against before.

In some ways it was an enormous mystery and confusingly indistinct. But the deeply rooted ache in his body couldn't be ignored or wished out of existence. Whatever else took place in his life, Zach knew with every certainty that TJ Reese was going to play a role in it.

TJ and her baby.

Doreen reappeared, wearing a bright smile. "I saw her for a few minutes and she's doing fine."

"You saw TJ?" Zach questioned eagerly. "What's taking so long?"

"It's only been four hours, Zachary." Doreen laughed. "Believe me, everything is going just like it should." She touched Zach's arm. "Jack and I can't hang around. We left the kids with a neighbor and have to get home. You might as well leave, too, Zachary. It could take hours yet.''

"Maybe. I'll see," Zach replied, knowing in his heart that he'd stay all night if necessary.

After Doreen and Jack had gone, Zach went to the cafeteria for an extra large cup of coffee to go. He returned to the maternity wing and settled down in a waiting area. However long it took, he was going to be here for TJ.

At 10:14 that night, TJ gave birth to a six-pound seven-ounce daughter. Within an hour, TJ was in a private room, feeling drowsy but elated. A nurse came in. "Mrs. Reese, I know it's late and you're tired, but Mr. Torelli has been here all afternoon. He's asked to see you for just a minute. We do bend the rules a trifle in maternity, and..."

"He's still here?" TJ stared at the nurse, her eyes wide with wonder. "You mean that he waited all this time?"

The nurse, who was young and pretty and pregnant herself, smiled warmly. "He certainly did. Shall I send him in?"

TJ drew a deep breath. "Yes, of course." She hadn't thought about Zach all afternoon, but then she hadn't thought much of anything beyond what was going on with her and Tina Rae Reese.

Tina Rae Reese, surely the most beautiful, perfect baby girl ever born. At the thought of her precious daughter, tears filled TJ's eyes. She was going to be a good mother. Tina would never lack love or necessities, not while she, TJ, drew breath.

The nurse had been gone only minutes when the door opened a few inches. TJ quickly wiped her eyes and smiled at Zach, who'd rather tentatively stuck his head through the crack. "Come in, Zach."

He sauntered the few steps to the bed in an offhanded way, while his expression looked somewhat abashed. "How're you doing?"

"All right," TJ said quietly. Her right hand rose to her hair as she quite suddenly realized that she must look a fright. Giving birth might be a lovely event idealistically, but its reality didn't leave a woman with many pretensions.

And she certainly hadn't been expecting visitors tonight, especially Zach.

"You're feeling okay, then?" he persisted softly. She looked so small in that austere white bed, very young, very innocent and totally unguarded. Nothing of her business capabilities showed in her face or form. She had just become a mother and that's what Zach felt from her, the warmth and gentleness of sweet and utter femaleness.

TJ smiled. "I'm a little tired. I had a girl, Zach. Did the nurse tell you?"

"Yeah, she did. A little girl. That's great, TJ, really great."

"She's beautiful. Have you seen her?"

He shook his head. "The nursery has been shuttered for hours. If I were the father..."

"Yes, of course," TJ said when his voice trailed off. Zach was no relation whatsoever, and while the staff in the maternity wing bent the hospital's generally stringent rules on visiting hours for new mothers, they couldn't possibly do the same for the newborns.

Zach was standing about a foot from the bed, looking a little uncomfortable. He wasn't sure of himself right now, TJ realized. A question clung in her mind: *Why did you stay all day?* But she couldn't ask it. The fact that he'd done it all on his own created more questions and a noticeable ambiguity: Part of her was grateful for an unsolicited kindness, and part of her was a bit uneasy about so much concern.

"I promised the nurse I wouldn't stay long. I'll come by tomorrow after work."

"Thanks for everything, Zach."

"No problem." He hesitated. "What's her name?"

"Tina Rae."

"That's pretty." He shifted his weight with indecision and then moved closer to the bed.

TJ's pupils grew larger. She was lying flat on her back, with a sheet and a soft cotton spread tucked around her. One light burned in the room, a wall lamp just over the bed.

Zach's expression was tender, his eyes dark with emotions TJ couldn't decipher. It seemed so strange that he would be here right now, intimate, somehow.

When he leaned over, TJ's lips parted for a surprised breath. His kiss on her cheek was nothing but gentle, but it sent shock waves throughout her system.

She didn't know what to say, and when he rose up and looked at her, she merely looked back in stunned silence. "Good night," he murmured softly, then walked away.

TJ closed her eyes as the door swung shut behind him. The hospital was quiet and felt almost eerie. *She* felt eerie, very alone, very sad. The tears slowly seeped from beneath her lashes and coursed down her temples to the pillow. She let them flow while admitting that she had no idea why she was weeping.

Maybe it was for Tommy and what might have been. Maybe for her tiny daughter, who would never know her father.

Maybe it was for Zach, who had waited for seven hours to spend three minutes with her. Or for herself, because she felt so confused.

The nurse came in again, this time carrying a small paper cup. "Take these tablets, Mrs. Reese."

TJ reached for a tissue and dried her eyes. The nurse smiled in understanding. "Feeling a little emotional? It happens sometimes after childbirth."

"A little. Is this your first pregnancy?" TJ glanced at the young woman's tummy while she raised herself up on an elbow.

"My second." She gave TJ the glass of water from the bed stand. "The blues will pass."

TJ swallowed the two small tablets. "I'm sure you're right." She lay back. "I'm just very tired."

"Of course you are. Good night, Mrs. Reese. Sleep well."

"Thank you." TJ snapped off the light. Outside lights filtering through the window cast pale gray shadows in the room. She didn't feel like crying any longer and her thoughts jumped around, to the business, to Tina Rae, to Zach.

His kiss had been startling. The man, himself, was startling. He did things she didn't anticipate, like staying here all afternoon. Had anyone ever done anything like that for her before? She had some good friends, but Zach's consideration went far beyond what one ordinarily expected from friends, and certainly beyond what an employer expected from an employee. Even Doreen, who was combination friend and employee, hadn't been able to ignore her own responsibilities to linger at the hospital all day, awaiting Tina's birth.

No indeed, no one had ever put themselves out for her as Zach Torelli had done today. Certainly not Tommy, not even during their happy times. She had always carried her own weight in the business, putting out as much effort as Tommy. More, in many instances. He had never tried to make her share of the load lighter, which hadn't bothered her at the time. Looking back, however, TJ realized that the reason she felt so keenly possessive of the business was because she was the one who had worried and stewed through problems during the initial years. And she'd been the one who had solved most of them, often by herself.

To be completely honest about the matter, Zach had already assumed a more serious responsibility than Tommy had ever accepted. Tommy would have spurts of conscientiousness and dive into some chore with enormous energy. But his input had never been steady and altogether reliable. Zach was the exact opposite.

But that observation was related to the business. What should she make of Zach's personal attentions?

Her thoughts went back to that moment when she had tied his kindness to his desire to own another construction company. The same quick and vehement denial she had experienced then rose again. But TJ knew the idea was there, embedded in her psyche all the same. Some small part of herself, however unwanted, would remain on guard with Zach. Her sense of self-protectiveness had become too well developed to eradicate suspicion from her system.

Sighing, TJ rolled to her side and faced the window. In this quiet, somber place, her unnerving physical reactions to Zach were more easily defined: He was an immensely attractive man, which any woman would appreciate.

But thinking, responsible women didn't allow themselves to ruin a necessary business liaison with personal involvement, and she desperately needed Zach's expertise in the next few months. She longed for time with her baby, yearned for nurturing days with Tina without worry about the business. She would have that wonderful freedom as long as Zach stayed in her employ as superintendent.

And muddying the situation with a romatic entanglement would be extremely shortsighted.

It was something she would have to get across to Zach without injuring his pride or damaging their working relationship—no small feat.

TJ closed her eyes and breathed in a long, weary breath. She would think about it again tomorrow. She was really too tired to continue attempting to assess the complex situation with any degree of intelligence tonight.

She fell asleep thinking of her beautiful baby daughter.

Six

Zach pulled the Wagoneer into TJ's driveway and turned off the ignition. His visits to her home had become routine during the past six weeks. TJ's appearances at the office were usually during the morning hours, when he was out on the job sites. To talk to her in person about the progress of the various projects, he had been coming to her house nearly every afternoon.

It was a pattern he liked, because it gave him the opportunity to see Tina along with TJ. He grinned broadly when TJ opened the door with the baby in her arms. Usually Tina was sleeping when he arrived and all he got was a peek at her in the nursery. Today she was bright-eyed and wide-awake.

TJ smiled indulgently. "She's playing games with her schedule today. Come on in."

Crossing the threshold, Zach closed the door. "She's all right, isn't she?"

"She's been a little fussy, but mainly I think she's just asserting herself." TJ smiled down at Tina. "We've been having a nice long chat. She's a wonderful listener."

Zach laughed at the image of a mother and daughter "chat" between these two. The sight of Tina in TJ's arms never failed to move him, anyway, but this was another of those special moments he'd been savoring of late.

Things hadn't been quite the same since Tina's birth. For one thing, TJ's physical appearance had changed so much he could hardly believe it. He'd thought her pretty and appealing before, but the woman she was now was keeping him awake nights.

Her waist had deflated to a mere handspan. Not without effort, he knew. TJ had mentioned an exercise program, which, in Zach's opinion, had certainly worked. Her bosom was firm and rounded, the curvature of her hips was prettily defined and her legs seemed longer—all because the size of her waist had decreased so much.

Another obvious change was with her eyes. That tired expression he'd seen so often was gone. In its place was contentment, joy, love. She was, without a doubt, the most desirable woman he'd ever known.

Standing beside her now, with Tina in her arms and all three of them surrounded by soft, female, powdery scents, Zach had to clench his teeth to stop himself from putting his arms around mother and child and just holding them.

But he knew it wouldn't end there. Just holding TJ wouldn't be nearly enough. He wanted her in the most elemental sense, much more than he'd ever wanted any woman.

"How about something to drink?" TJ asked brightly, having become a little too aware of Zach standing so close. They never had had that talk she'd thought about in the hospital, the one about keeping things cool between them. An appropriate time for such a discussion hadn't arisen. Zach had confined his affection—if that's what he felt for her—to admiring looks.

TJ was grateful he hadn't pressured her. She was beginning to worry that if he ever did, she might lose her grasp on common sense. She liked Zach with a depth that demanded caution, and it seemed essential to her that they keep their interaction on a liking-only basis.

It was Saturday afternoon and Zach felt like relaxing a little. He'd been working hard for weeks now, with the almost daily visits to TJ's home his only distraction.

"I'd like a cold beer if you have one handy," he told her.

"Sure do. In the refrigerator. Why don't you help yourself?"

"Thanks."

"I'll be in the living room."

Zach walked into the living room a minute later with a bottle of beer. TJ was sitting in a rocker and Tina looked drowsy in her mother's arms. TJ spoke quietly. "Usually she goes right to sleep with her bottle. But she drank it today and stayed awake."

"She's getting sleepy now." Zach sat on the sofa. He would never tire of looking at TJ holding Tina. Like her mother, the infant had light hair. She was a pretty baby and getting prettier every day. Zach could see TJ in the child. He couldn't remember Tommy's features well enough to recognize them in his daughter, but that really didn't matter. Tina was TJ's baby, and that's all that counted for him.

"So," TJ murmured. "How did it go today?"

Zach began a narration of the day's events. The company had landed the contract on that forty-unit development TJ had analyzed before Tina's birth, and the off-site utilities work had already been completed, along with the cement slabs for the houses. Basements were rare things in Las Vegas, as they were in Arizona and many other desert areas. Caliche was the main reason. The substance was a crusted calcium carbonate found in dry regions and it was as hard as granite, very costly to dig through.

They discussed the project for about ten minutes, then TJ smiled down at her sleeping baby. "Time for bed," she whispered with a small smile at Zach.

He finished his beer while TJ was gone, enjoying the peace and comfort of her house. TJ had not yet returned to full-time work. She spent two or three mornings a week at the office and dropped in spontaneously beyond that. Obviously Doreen and Jim were keeping everything on an even keel in administration, while he, as super, was handling the physical end of the business. The arrangement seemed to be working well, and Zach could see no reason why TJ should hurry back to total immersion in the operation.

She belongs right here with the baby, he thought, admitting that he was a lot more old-fashioned about mothers and children than he'd known before Tina's birth. TJ would probably become indignant if he should mention his opinion. He had little right to voice such opinions, after all.

Which was becoming harder to swallow every day.

He frowned while recalling that he'd done nothing about his decision to gain TJ's personal trust. On an employer-employee basis, they couldn't get alone any better than they did. But that little kiss he'd given her at the hospital was the most personal thing that had passed between them.

It was time to do something about the situation, if he was ever going to.

Feeling a zing of excitement in his blood, Zach got up and went to the kitchen for another beer. He placed the empty bottle in TJ's recycling container and took a fresh one from the refrigerator. Instead of going back to the living room, he leaned his hips against the sink counter and waited for TJ.

This was not a spur-of-the-moment decision for him, although it seemed like one. His feelings for TJ had been growing and expanding from their first meeting. She liked him, too. A man would have to be completely dense not to understand the subtle message in TJ's smiles.

But she also had the ability to make him slightly tongue-tied, and Zach couldn't pretend any sort of macho nonchalance while he awaited TJ's appearance.

She came in after a few minutes. "Oh, there you are! I thought you might have left."

"No, I'm still here."

TJ heard something peculiar in Zach's voice. Her gaze became curious. He was big and handsome and sexy, and those qualities, for some unknown reason, had become more apparent during her brief absence. Her pulse was suddenly beating ridiculously fast. She'd known this moment was coming for a long time, but preparing for it had been impossible. "Is...something wrong?" she questioned weakly, knowing all too well that a flush was warming her face and throat.

The flush elated Zach. She knew how she affected him and that she was much more than a boss to him. She *knew!* They had actually just communicated on a very meaningful level, something he didn't have the power or the desire to ignore. The time *was* right for a personal overture; he knew that now.

"I'd like to take you out to dinner tonight," he said with a little half smile. "To a nice place."

TJ's heart skipped a beat. A dinner invitation from anyone shouldn't unnerve her, but there was a lot more behind this one than a wish to share a meal in a nice place.

"Oh. Well, I haven't left Tina at night yet. I'm not sure Daisy could come over on such short notice." Daisy Holcomb was the very reliable woman TJ entrusted Tina with during her trips to the office. Not just anyone would do, either, certainly not someone she didn't know extremely well.

TJ was trying not to look at him, Zach saw. And her every syllable was an evasion. He didn't believe she was into game playing, so her discomfort was genuine. But somehow he had to get them beyond their present relationship. A little shock therapy might do it, he figured.

He deliberately stared at her body, slowly, letting her know that he was admiring her breasts, her legs, every inch of her. It was a bold, sizzling look, intentionally so. For the first time since they'd met, he wanted her to feel the full impact of their chemistry, the import of her own femininity and what it did to him.

TJ was having trouble with a regular breathing pattern. Her clothing was a black-and-white-checked skirt, a white blouse and black toeless slippers. The outfit was becoming but hardly seductive, and Zach was making her feel as if she were wearing filmy lingerie. For two people who hadn't even shared a real kiss, there was an incredible amount of electricity in the air.

Zach set down the bottle of beer on the counter and took a step toward TJ. Her eyes widened and she backed up. "We... you... Zach, please," she stammered in a near whisper. Her heart was thudding unmercifully, making coherent thought difficult.

"Don't be upset. I've got to speak plainly. I've thought and thought about it, and there's no other way. I want you, TJ." He took another step.

She swallowed hard. "But..."

"I've pretended for over two months now. Should I go on pretending? Tell me. Should I keep burying my feelings?"

"I... Zach, this... could change everything."

"I would hope so." She had stopped backing away, which was encouraging. It was out in the open at last, giving Zach tremendous relief. But the relief was momentary, fleeting, quickly being replaced by desire. He'd never ached for a woman for two months before, and the tension in his body was demanding some sort of surcease.

TJ's mind was like a blank canvas. She knew that her baby slept in the nursery and that this was Zach in her kitchen. But she didn't seem able to think beyond that, not clearly, certainly not with any of the finely turned precision she normally used on a problem.

A dram of clarity infiltrated her confusion. Yes, this was a problem, a monumental problem, if one wanted to get down to hard facts.

Getting down to hard facts, however, seemed very unpleasant in the face of so much emotion. Rather coldhearted, too. Where Zach was concerned, she was anything but cold, she was forced to admit. The man was weakening her knees, and he hadn't even touched her.

But he was going to. Oh, yes, he was definitely going to.

What's more, she wanted his touch. Her system was being stormed by rippling, sensual aches and an insistent restlessness. She'd noticed those feelings around Zach before, but she'd always done her best to ignore them.

Now she didn't want to ignore them. A dim thought flitted through her mind. Wasn't this what she'd been afraid of,
that if he ever pressured her, she wouldn't have the will-
power to resist? It was happening . . . right now . . . and her
own body wasn't cooperating with her previous intentions
to steer clear of this kind of encounter.

With Zach so close, it actually felt like someone else's
decision. TJ's tongue flicked and dampened her lips. Zach's
right hand rose slowly. His fingertips played with her hair.
His eyes were dark and leveled on hers. "You're so pretty,
TJ."

"Am I?" She felt pretty right now, but truly believed that
compared to Zach's outstanding looks, hers were only ordinary. He was beautiful, long and lean and completely
masculine. His jeans and white shirt fit his lithe physique to
perfection. His gorgeous dark skin and flashing blue eyes
were exceptionally striking.

More important than every one of his many physical at-
tributes, he reached a very private and personal part of her,
something she had wondered about ever risking again. It
was the part of her that Tommy had nearly destroyed, and
entrusting it to another man was frightening.

But emotional control at the moment was almost laugh-
able. Zach's personality and aura were bombarding her
senses. His unique scent filled her lungs. Her very pores
seemed to be absorbing his masculine essence.

His hands moved to her shoulders and then gently urged
her forward. He'd said it so distinctly—*I want you, TJ.* No
man had ever said that to her before, not in those words. It
was shocking, yes, but it was also extremely stimulating.

They stared into each other's eyes. TJ put her hands on
his chest and slowly slid them upward. She could feel his
strong heartbeat and hear her own. She shouldn't be doing
this. She should maintain a working relationship with Zach,
nothing more.

And then one of his hands was deep in her hair, while his
other arm encircled her waist. His mouth came down on
hers, very gently at first, but almost immediately with un-

leashed hunger. The melding of their lips dizzied her. The sensation of his body burning into hers dazed her even more. They were pressed tightly together. The embrace was neither calm nor steady. In mere seconds, it had evolved to gasping, quick, needful kisses. She felt his tongue on her lips and in her mouth. His hands were roaming her body, touching, reaching, heating.

TJ recognized the astounding difference between kissing Zach and kissing anyone else. She wasn't trying to dwell on any such crass statistics, but it was so glaringly true that no man had ever made her feel so liquid and limp before. Emotions and feelings she hadn't even known she possessed were controlling her system, and they weren't all pleasurable.

In fact, this overwhelming wanting wasn't pleasurable at all! Breathing hard, TJ pushed herself free of Zach's arms.

The abrupt change of pace surprised him and he let her slip away. He read denial on her face, and a strange sort of embarrassment. "TJ..."

"No. No! Zach, we're not going to...to..."

"Make love?" he asked softly. "It's been between us right from the first, TJ."

"While I was pregnant?" She tried to scoff, to show disdain for the idea.

"Are you saying you didn't know? That you never sensed my feelings or felt anything yourself?"

"I felt...feel...Zach, I like you. I liked you right away. But this kind of involvement..." Her voice stopped. She took several small agitated steps, while her hands nervously smoothed her hair. "It...it's just not sensible."

Zach wondered if he'd heard right. She had kissed him back. She had leaned into him—he could still feel the imprint of her body on his—and she'd backed off because the incredibly deep feelings between them weren't "sensible"?

"Well...is it?" TJ questioned with a touch of acerbity.

Her pique was as annoying as her definition of sensibility. Zach picked up the bottle of beer and swallowed a mouthful. His pulse hadn't slowed down yet. As worked up as he'd gotten, it might not return to its normal rate in a month.

She had never annoyed him before. This was the first time they had ever really locked horns. Any differences of opinion on the business had always been easily and comfortably talked through.

There was neither ease nor comfort in the air right now.

"I'm not going to try and talk you into anything," Zach finally stated bluntly. "But I'd really like to hear why you think anything except a working relationship for you and me isn't sensible."

He'd spoken tensely. TJ's inner self recoiled. If her attitude alienated Zach, everything could fall apart. She wasn't ready to go back to work full-time and leave Tina all day, every day with a sitter, not even with Daisy Holcomb. Lately she'd even found herself wondering how long it would be before she *would* feel comfortable about leaving Tina for the kind of hours she used to put in on the business.

TJ attempted to calm her fluttering interior. She cleared her throat and rearranged her expression into one not quite so telling. "Maybe 'sensible' isn't the right word. What I meant was that we *are* working together, and..." She saw how his jaw was clenching. "Dammit, Zach, I can't pretend the company isn't important!"

"You can't pretend, but I can. Is that it?"

She had never seen him angry or even mildly irritated with her before, and she didn't know how to proceed. Before he'd entered her life, she'd been overworked and worried.

But she hadn't been helpless, and that's how she suddenly felt. She'd been leaning on him pretty heavily. Not just him; Doreen and Jim were doing all of the paperwork, the bidding, the project analyses. Her input since Tina's birth was minor compared to her former dedication. Regardless of anyone else's contribution, though, Zach had become the backbone of the company, its real strength, and the thought of losing him right now was soul sickening. Even with his plans to have his own company again, she'd been counting on him to be with her for several months yet.

"Zach, I need you." Her voice was husky, although she'd tried very hard to keep a plea out of it. She only wanted him to know how she felt, not sound like she was begging.

"I need you, too."

"But you're talking about...!"

"Yes, I am." Zach looked away from her stricken face for a moment, then placed the beer bottle on the counter and moved closer to her. She stood there and watched him coming, unable to do anything else. He put a hand on the side of her face and then moved it very slowly, as if memorizing the curve and texture of her cheek, the silkiness of her hairline. "What do you think I want from you, TJ?"

Her gaze darted from his and back again. "I...well, you've made that rather clear, haven't you?"

"We're both adults. Why is wanting each other so upsetting to you?"

"It's...very complicated."

Zach's hand became still as his eyes narrowed. "Is it because I'm just another employee?"

"No! Of course not!"

"I'm not always going to be working for someone else."

"I know—God, I *know!*" TJ swung away, breaking contact with the hand that had felt so good on her cheek. "You don't understand. I don't have any...I don't even know what to call it. Prejudice? Is that what you're insinuating? Your working for me doesn't have anything to do with...oh, what am I saying! Of course it has something to do with my attitude. But not in the way you're thinking."

Zach was dealing—or trying to deal—with a knotted core of pain in his gut. He couldn't have been this mistaken about TJ's feelings. All along he'd picked up things from her, a private smile, a special light in her green eyes, a female expression on her pretty face, silent messages that he'd interpreted as uniquely theirs.

Anyway, the whole thing was gnawing a hole in him. He growled in a not very friendly voice, "So my thinking's been all cockeyed. Well, suppose you straighten me out."

TJ had been moving around. Finding herself beside the kitchen table, she sat on the very edge of it, a rather precarious perch with the toes of her slippers against the floor.

She ardently hoped that she looked less tense than she felt. Maybe it was wrong to be so focused on only one path, but how did anyone really know what was a mistake in judgment and what wasn't?

She could only do what she *thought* was best. Her chin came up slightly. "There just isn't room in my life right now for a man. We're friends, Zach, good friends. I'd like to keep it at that."

Zach swallowed a bitter retort. Yes, they were friends. But the groping, hungry kisses they'd just shared far surpassed mere friendship.

"Zach, you know how much I depend on you. Without you on the job..." TJ sighed. "You know the situation as well as I do."

He looked at her, his gaze lingering on her sweet, sexy mouth. She was trying to kid him right along with herself. Not in a teasing way. She was deadly serious. She actually believed that a personal tie would destroy their working relationship. More disturbing to him, she thought that a verbal denial would cool the heat between them.

It wouldn't. Nothing would. Nothing except some very hot lovemaking. And even then, Zach felt, the fire would flare up again almost immediately. This wasn't some trivial, short-lived passion between them. It had sparked at their first meeting and expanded daily. And it wasn't all sex and sin, either. They genuinely liked each other. They could talk for hours. Granted, their conversations had been mostly about the business. But whatever the topic, they knew how to communicate.

Right now, though, their entire relationship seemed cloudy and indistinct. A few minutes of intimacy had sent them both into a tailspin, and neither of them was handling it very well.

He wasn't going to back off and leave the matter dangling. Not until she at least admitted that more was going on between them than friendship.

Moving to the table, Zach pulled out the chair closest to TJ and slowly sank down on it. He didn't touch her, but he was near enough to feel her warmth. Color flared in her cheeks, but he had to give her credit: She stood her ground.

His very nearness was a threat, TJ realized weakly. A threat to her determination. He wasn't going to let her off the hook. Maybe his kindness had come to an end. The possibility didn't surprise her. Since Tommy's infractions and infidelities had really sunk in, she had been likening men to chameleons, anyway. They charmed to get what they wanted. Once attained, their true colors weren't always pretty.

Zach's eyes were guarded, slightly hooded. "So, all you want from me is friendship."

"Yes," she whispered.

"And to maintain the status quo."

"Yes."

"And you didn't kiss me back."

TJ's eyes widened. "I . . . suppose I did, but you took me by surprise."

"Oh, I see. Surprise results in response for you." Zach lifted his hand to her waist. "Are you surprised right now?" His hand lazily drifted downward, resting finally on her thigh.

"You're not going to leave it alone, are you?" TJ whispered unsteadily, deeply shaken by the tide of warmth washing over her. His caress was suggestive, meant to arouse, and it was working. Her insides were oozing together again, getting all hot and squishy.

"Lighten up, honey," he murmured softly. "The thought of making love shouldn't make you look like the end of the world is imminent."

He had succeeded in startling her again. "Lighten up" was exactly what he'd just done. How he'd made such a speedy transition from almost lethal sobriety to subtle

amusement was a total mystery, but it no doubt was another of those chameleon changes inherent in his gender.

That whole theory hurt when applied to Zach, however,
and TJ didn't dwell on it. Besides, she had other concerns
right now, the aching, insistent yearning in her own body,
for one. Zach was blatantly offering her thrills beyond any
she had ever experienced, and risking her whole way of life
and her financial security on electric blue eyes and sexual
excitement was insane.

But the desire to do so was becoming overwhelming. TJ
felt herself trembling, a reaction to Zach's proximity and the
big hand on her thigh. Its movement was barely percepti-
ble, just enough to keep her reminded of its presence.

There was a hopelessness to the situation. She not only
needed him on the job, she wanted him in her bed. How
long could she maintain a reconcilable distance between the
two conflicting attitudes?

TJ's eyes closed. Her heart was thudding in her chest. She
felt boxed in, trapped by her own weakness for this man. He
was one hundred percent right about it happening at their
first meeting. She'd known it, even if she had refused to
admit it.

Zach looked grim. "Com'ere," he growled, and deftly
pulled her down on his lap. "You're unhappy, and that
wasn't my intention." She didn't fight the embrace; she
simply didn't have the strength. Instead, her head wilted into
the hollow of his throat and shoulder, while his arms curved
around her.

She couldn't remember the last time she'd sat on a man's
lap. There was so much to it, the sensation of firm but
yielding flesh, a distinctly masculine chest, the configura-
tion of male thighs and arms. It felt heavenly, to be honest,
like security and protection.

But it was also very sexy. Her right hip connected with the
front of his jeans, and she couldn't pretend not to recognize Zach's state of arousal. She was much more adult than
she'd been when Tommy had courted her. The past few
years had put her through an emotional wringer, evoking the

worst kind of despair and an almost euphoric bliss. Tina was the cause of the bliss; Tommy had caused the despair.

And now there was Zach, and he caused some of every conceivable emotion. There was only one that warranted no debate: He made her feel like a woman.

His hands gently stroked her back. "I don't want to pressure you into anything, TJ, but . . ."

"But you could if you tried," she interjected, noting the catch in her voice that gave it a husky, breathy quality.

"I don't affect you any stronger than you affect me. I only want you to face that."

"I'm facing it."

"But you don't like it."

"It scares me."

He tugged her head back to see her face. "Why?"

She searched the blue depths of his eyes. "A lot of reasons—the business, Tina, my marriage, the future. Zach, I'm not ready for a personal commitment."

He looked long and hard at her. "Can we take those reasons one at a time?"

"Zach . . ." There was that note of helplessness again. She was worrying and it was in her voice.

"We have to talk about it," he said quietly.

"I'm not against discussion, but I'm very confused right now." She was. Being in his arms was clouding her mind. The worry was clear-cut, even through the haze of sexuality melting her physical self. But everything else was whirling and chaotic.

"All right, if we can't talk, can we do this?" His mouth touched hers for a moment, sending a shock wave through her that resulted in a head-to-toe shiver. "Tell me what to do," he whispered. "I'm burning up for you, TJ."

She was burning, too. Every cell of her body felt as if it were on fire. He took her chin and held it and looked deeply into her eyes. "Kiss me," he whispered. "The way you want to, the way I want you to. Forget everything but what's happening right this minute. It's not a crime to want someone. We're a lot more to each other than what we've been living with. We always were, right from the first. Stop denying it, or wishing it out of existence. It's not going to go away, not my feelings, not yours.''

His eyes looked like liquid blue fire. ''I promise not to go further than you want, but kiss me, TJ. Put your arms around my neck and kiss me.''

Seven

He was so appealing. Everything female in TJ seemed to magnify in response. A thought flitted through her mind while her hands locked behind Zach's head: He had said he wouldn't pressure her, but that's what he was doing.

But then nothing seemed to matter very much beyond the rushing of her own blood.

She placed her lips on his. His head moved slowly, which made the kiss deliciously sensual. Giving in to Zach's logic was foolhardy, but in scrupulous self-analysis, she had never strayed from a rather straight and narrow path her entire life.

Well, she'd lost the battle to maintain her rigid standards. She wanted things from Zach that had never even entered her mind before meeting him. A virgin's curiosity fired her imagination. The hardness in his jeans excited her, his hands on her body made her want to moan and writhe against him.

The first kiss melted into another. It asked more of her and TJ was willing to give it. Her tongue moved into his mouth. Zach's arms tightened around her. She had given him the green light, and what reason was there not to heed it?

There was none. They were both unattached, both free to explore this wildly exciting aspect of their relationship. It was what Zach had wanted for a long time, and he felt nothing amiss in taking it to its obvious conclusion.

He stroked her hair, her back. She felt so good on his lap, her warmth penetrating clothes and skin, reaching even his bones. She smelled like heaven on earth, a unique scent that had been tantalizing his senses for two months.

At the waistband of her skirt, he tugged her blouse loose and slipped a hand up under it. The skin of her back was silky and hot. She wriggled at the caress, and Zach's whole system jumped at the sensation of her breasts moving against his chest.

He thought of her bed. That's where they should be right now, on a bed. He wanted to undress her, to see her, to touch her. He wanted so much, probably more than was humanly possible, but his imagination was devising disturbingly erotic images. With TJ in his arms, the thought of making love to fulfillment caused more than the normal physical reactions. His insides were molten with desire, but also with caring, with affection. TJ cared for him, too; he could feel it in the way she was kissing him.

His lips left hers to trail down her throat. He was breathing in jerks and starts. His heart was practically bursting in his chest. Under her blouse, he unhooked the clasp of her bra and then slid his hand around her slender torso to a breast. It was arousingly full, and soft except for its firm, puckered crest. Becoming greedier, he moved to the other breast, and then back and forth.

"Zach..." His name was a gasp in her throat. She had never become totally submerged in lovemaking before, and she could feel herself sinking deeper and deeper into emotion.

Her unsteady hands moved over him, his muscular neck
and shoulders, his thick, dense hair. She was curious and
couldn't touch him enough.

"Your room," Zach mumbled hoarsely. Their confinement on the chair was getting uncomfortable, the restric-
tions of clothing and space becoming intolerable.

"Pardon?"

"Let's go to your room." He nibbled at her lower lip,
finding it delectable. He wanted to nibble elsewhere, to taste
her breasts, her thighs, the very essence of her femininity.

His words and their meaning reverberated in TJ's brain,
and she experienced a strange sense of withdrawal. Or
maybe it wasn't so strange. Wasn't such abandoned behavior much stranger for her than control?

Zach raised his head to see her face. He'd been moving
fast, and he realized this was all a little sudden for TJ.
Kisses, yes. Caresses and petting, fine. But the bedroom? He
was going to have to cool down by himself today. As worked
up as TJ had gotten, she wasn't quite ready for the final
step.

He attempted a smile and knew it had to look pretty grim.
"There's no hurry. I got a little carried away, but we don't
have to rush into anything." He touched her hair and then
tenderly tucked one side of it behind her ear. "At least you
know how I feel about you now."

Did she? TJ stared into his eyes. Her stomach was tied in
almost crippling knots. Of course the bedroom was the log-
ical conclusion to the kind of kisses they'd just indulged in.
Why had his suggestion shocked her?

It was because of her own uncertainties, wasn't it? She
was a big girl and knew where playing with fire led, where
sitting on a man's lap and kissing him and fooling around
the way they'd been doing could end up.

There was something else, though. This wasn't *all* shock
and surprise. She'd known from the beginning that something was brewing between her and Zach. The biggest
drawback to acceptance was circumstance—her circumstance, in particular.

And mistrust and suspicion and an awful lot of self-doubt. "I'm sorry," she whispered unsteadily. She couldn't be unkind, regardless of so much ambiguity. "Maybe I just need a little time to get used to...you know...this sort of thing between us."

"It's really up to you, TJ. You know what I want for us."

Maybe that was the bind, what Zach wanted. He was a fantastic employee, but his goal was much higher. How far would he go to attain it?

The thought sickened TJ, as it always did. Besides, she had a few questions about her own participation in this overwhelming encounter. Was she really ready for another serious relationship? She knew she couldn't have any other kind, and why would she ever trust her own instincts with a man again? One bad marriage should be enough for anyone. She had a daughter to raise, a business to run, and maybe that's all she needed.

"I better get up." Her voice was thin and reedy. Staying on Zach's lap when she knew she wasn't going to the bedroom with him was only teasing him, and she wasn't a woman who deliberately teased.

His hand curved around the back of her head. "All right, but first..." His mouth settled on hers in a slow-burning kiss that curled her toes. She had to forcibly stop herself from wrapping her arms around his neck again, from pressing into him.

From just giving in completely.

Zach broke the kiss and gazed into her eyes. "You look confused. Don't be, not about us."

Gathering what little strength she could, TJ slipped off his lap. Her hands fluttered over her clothing. "Easy to say," she said huskily. "Excuse me for a few minutes. I'm going to check on Tina."

Zach watched her dart from the kitchen and let his head fall back with a long frustrated sigh. Then he got up and did a little pacing. He hurt in a particularly sensitive area of his body. The hurting would stop, of course. No man ever died from not finishing something he'd started.

And he'd definitely started something with TJ today.

Zach smiled faintly. At least it was out in the open. The feelings and emotions just simmering beneath the surface for two months, both his and TJ's, were finally unveiled, and that felt good to him. Very good.

TJ reached up under her blouse and hooked her bra, next tucking the blouse's tails back into her skirt. The bathroom mirror reflected her almost gaunt expression. She felt that she'd become mired in some kind of emotional morass, and she had no idea what to do about it.

If she returned to the kitchen and told Zach even a small portion of the turmoil in her mind, he'd probably walk off the job.

Or would he? Lord, she didn't know what to think.

And just why should the idea of Zach leaving the company send icy shivers up her spine? She'd managed without him before, she could certainly do so again.

It wouldn't be easy. She would have to leave Tina with Daisy until she found another supervisor. The projects would become hopelessly snarled without diligent supervision. Zach had promised to take care of locating another man before he left to open his own business, but if he went out of anger, he'd probably wash his hands of the obligation.

TJ studied her face in the mirror. Her responses to Zach had been disturbingly real. Those hot, steamy feelings were still alive in her body, for that matter, proof of their reality. But why had she allowed his very first advance when she'd been so adamantly opposed to any such familiarity between them?

She searched her own eyes, looking for truth, for something to hang on to. Wanting a man's kisses seemed to mean very little in the larger scheme of things. For one thing, the notion that Zach might do just about anything to control his own company again would not disappear. Reese Home Builders was established and successful. A good reputation was like money in the bank in the construction business.

Developers came to her. If she ever decided to expand, it would be a simple matter. More employees, of course, more work, more tension, more responsibility. But an ambitious, intelligent man like Zach had to have seen the company's potential by now.

Yet those suspicions were tough to accept with any degree of conviction. They were, after all, nothing but supposition and darned weak at that. TJ was blasted with guilt every time they infiltrated other thoughts. But she was no raving beauty and Zach was—in a distinctly masculine way, of course. She was discovering an abysmal lack of confidence in herself beyond a business sense, which was a disheartening blow on top of everything else.

The situation was very complex. She had come to believe in something unusual, Zach's indispensability, when she'd never before given the word much credence. But he'd made things so easy for her in the past two months, and no one ever had. Without someone as good—which she'd had no luck in finding before Zach had answered her ad—she would have to dig in and all but abandon Tina.

Of course, "abandoning" Tina was an exaggeration. But she felt prone to exaggeration right now. Nothing was simple, certainly.

TJ washed her face, applied a little makeup and brushed her hair. Reasonably put back together, she peeked into the nursery and saw that Tina was sleeping peacefully. The tiny girl's favorite position was on her tummy, and her diapered bottom made an endearing little bump in the pink cotton blanket TJ had lightly draped around her earlier.

Tears stung TJ's eyes. She didn't want to go back to work full-time and leave her baby in someone else's care. Not yet. In another few weeks or a month, maybe, but not right now. She hadn't known she would feel so strongly about this. Her job ordinarily consisted of very long hours and tremendous responsibility. Other people were presently handling the operation with only partial input from her. She wanted to keep it that way, and she could, as long as Zach stayed with the company.

By Zach's own timetable, he would be with her for another four or five months. It would be imprudent and totally irresponsible for her to do anything to shorten that
program.

She was not going to slide into an affair with Zach, and
she was going to have to make him see that today's misstep
was the end of it, without hurting his pride.

Tiptoeing away, with her own heart aching, TJ admitted
that her feelings where Zach was concerned were badly
muddled. More than that, there were facets to her personality that she was just beginning to grasp as a part of herself. The past few years had changed her, and she hadn't
realized how much.

She was a person now who would stop and think before
doing anything, and she had Tommy to either thank or curse
for so much caution.

TJ found Zach on the back patio. It was shaded with a
solid roof and overlooked the pool. Large ceramic pots
contained red-orange geraniums and bright yellow mari-
golds. As was the custom in Vegas, the entire backyard was
enclosed by a high cement-block wall. One could hear
neighbors occasionally, but most backyards were completely out of sight.

Leaving the kitchen door ajar in case Tina should wake
up, TJ stepped outside. Zach got to his feet with a softly
spoken "Hi."

"Hi." Why was her heart in her throat from just looking
at him? This was mad. Why couldn't she control her own
damned pulse rate!

"I should probably be going, but I didn't want to leave
without letting you know."

"Thank you." TJ's head was beginning to ache. The
stress of so much wanting, wondering and worrying was
bound to catch up with a person, she reasoned.

"TJ...about tonight. Is there any chance of that dinner
out together?"

"Probably not. I've never discussed evening hours with Daisy. I know I should give her more notice."

"How about tomorrow night? We could catch a show, if you'd like. There are some big stars in town."

There were always famous people playing Vegas—singers, dancers, comedians. Almost any night of the year, one could see an excellent show at any number of casinos.

But the glitz and glamour of the big shows didn't entice TJ in the least. The crowds were horrendous and the prices skyrocketing. As for gambling, forget it. She wouldn't put a coin in a machine or sit at a blackjack table for anything. After years of living in Nevada, she had seen so many people lose so much of their hard-earned money, she wasn't even tempted to try her luck.

So had Zach. After his tragic experience with his cousin, Zach wasn't apt to be inviting her out for an evening of gambling.

No, his invitation was aimed entirely at getting them to spend time together, away from business, away from any of their ordinary routines. And that's where the danger lay, of course. It was nothing short of rash for the two of them to even consider dating.

"I really don't care to go near the Strip," TJ said quietly. "Downtown, either."

"I understand. There are a lot of good restaurants we could try, though."

"Yes, I know."

"Will you talk to your sitter about tomorrow night?"

An evening in a good restaurant had a certain amount of appeal. It had been ages since she'd eaten anything except home cooking or fast food, and Daisy would probably agree to an evening engagement. It could all be arranged, TJ knew deep down.

But she simply did not want to leave Tina at night yet, however reliable Daisy was. It was bad enough during the day, and wasn't she doing everything she could to even avoid that?

TJ accepted the fact that she was just a little bit fanatic about Tina. Maybe more than a little, to be perfectly honest. But her baby was only six weeks old. Many new mothers had to return to their jobs much sooner than that, she knew. She was very fortunate to already have had these weeks at home.

But it was exactly that good fortune she wanted to preserve and protect, and wouldn't most women stay home with their babies if they could?

There was more than Tina in her mind, however. Going out with Zach was not wise. They had to see each other on an almost daily basis, but they didn't have to spend their evenings together.

"Thank you for the invitation, but I'm not very comfortable at the thought of leaving Tina at night yet. She's so small and defenseless, and...well, please understand, but I have to be here for her."

She had used the one excuse Zach couldn't debate. But the bottom line was, she was refusing to see him socially. He thought of pointing out that they could have dinner together right here, but that suggestion would have to come from her.

He tried not to count this as a strikeout. She wasn't immune to him, even if she wished she were. If he kissed her again right now, she would kiss him back. And if he wasn't already in more agony than anyone deserved, he would prove it, too.

No, it was over for today. He'd made his move and even some headway, but TJ wasn't easy in any sense of the word. Maybe anything worth having wasn't easy to attain, but why did he have to fall for a lady with so many hang-ups?

Right this second, that vulnerable sad look was back in her eyes, and it made him feel like a jerk to realize that he'd caused it.

"I better be going," he muttered. He was shaken over her attitude and couldn't help it. He'd expected more from her, more openness, less restraint. All these weeks of working together had seemed so special, and now he was wondering.

TJ followed him through the kitchen door and then the house. At the front door he paused and looked at her. "Should I come by tomorrow afternoon?"

"Are you working tomorrow?"

"The framers are starting on the Hanson project in the morning, and I intend being there."

TJ put an anxious hand on his arm. "Zach, I don't want today to ruin what we had. Feel free to come by whenever you need to talk to me, just like you've been doing."

"Thanks." If the word sounded a trifle forced and clipped, he couldn't help that, either. He opened the door. "See you tomorrow."

TJ closed it behind him, then weakly leaned against its cool, varnished surface. Had he been angry? Hurt? Egos were such damnably fragile things, and she wasn't all that practiced at stroking a man's.

"Surprise!" Doreen laughed when TJ opened the door that evening. "If I'm interrupting anything, just say so."

"No, of course not. I'm glad to see you. Come in."

"How's the munchkin?"

They walked into TJ's living room. "She's sleeping. She got off her usual schedule today."

"It happens," Doreen replied nonchalantly, and flopped down into a big chair.

"Want something to drink?"

"No, thanks. I can't stay long. The kids are with Jack. I want to get home in time to kiss them good-night." Doreen had been staring. "Are you feeling all right? You look a little peaked."

TJ's first impulse, as usual, was to say she was fine and not to worry about her. Doreen was such a fussbudget sometimes, but she was a good friend, and if TJ couldn't talk to a good friend about Zach, who could she talk to?

She sat on the sofa. "Can you take a few minutes to hear a very confused story?"

Doreen's left eyebrow shot up. "Something's going on. I knew it! I told Jack before I left the house that I had an odd feeling about you. First of all, tell me that you and Tina are both healthy."

Laughing shortly, TJ gave her head a shake. "It's nothing like that. Tina and I are both in very good health."

Doreen visibly relaxed. "Great. I'm ready to hear anything in that case. Shoot!"

TJ tried to settle back. She felt as tight as a coiled spring, though, and it wasn't any surprise that Doreen's bright eyes had spotted something peaked in her appearance. "It has to do with Zach," she said in a small voice.

"With Zachary? Our resident superhunk?" Doreen's gamine face lit up. "What'd he do, make a pass?"

Sighing, TJ put her head back. "Yes."

Doreen leaned forward with a triumphant expression. "I *told* you he liked you!"

"I'm not sure this has anything to do with affection. Doreen, Zach wants to own his own construction company again."

"Oh, no! When, TJ? Is this an immediate plan?"

"Therein lies the bind." TJ got off the sofa and moved about the room. She turned and faced her friend after a moment. "He talked about it right away. I just didn't say anything."

"Then you've known all along."

TJ felt Doreen's scrutiny. Her friend's wheels were obviously turning at full speed as she added up Zach's "pass" and career plans. "What connection are you making between his personal interest and his hope of owning his own company again?" Doreen finally inquired bluntly.

"Doreen, this might sound odd, but I've been wondering if Zach would..." TJ ran her fingers through her hair, nervously pushing it back from her face.

"Would what, TJ? What's bothering you?"

TJ drew a deep breath, than spoke quickly. "Is he capable of kissing up to me to get a shot at the company?"

"What?" The aghast expression on Doreen's face was as genuine as any TJ had ever seen. "TJ, you can't mean that!"

Embarrassment stuck TJ in an almost debilitating wave. She shouldn't have mentioned her suspicion to anyone, not when she had nothing to base it on except that nasty, insistent little mouse nibbling at her insides. She held up a hand. "I'm sorry. Forget it."

"No, wait a minute. It isn't like you to say something so negative about a person. You must have a reason. *Is* Zachary... how did you put it? ... kissing up to you?"

"He ... wants..."

"You?"

"Yes."

"How do you feel about him?"

If she thought about it, TJ could still feel his mouth on hers, his arms around her, the texture of his skin, the urgency in his body. The sexual attraction she felt for him was indisputable.

But that startling sizzle could be because she hadn't been kissed in a long time and maybe not enough even then. She could be ripe for an affair. She had an ego, too, after all, and maybe the damage hers had suffered during Tommy's feckless carousing was emerging.

Doreen knew a lot about Reese family history, but TJ couldn't bring herself to inject Tommy into the conversation. Her theory was only speculation, anyway. She didn't really know why she responded to a man she didn't quite trust. Maybe worse, though, she didn't trust her own instincts with the opposite sex. Zach made her feel warm and womanly and needful of a man's attentions—but so had Tommy at one time.

"I like Zach, of course," she admitted cautiously, which, surprisingly, was still as true as it had always been. Having had to face him on a whole different level of emotion hadn't altered her fondness of him.

"So do I," Doreen said dryly. "So does Jim. Everyone in the company likes him. Is that what we're talking about, how likable Zachary is?"

TJ was wishing she hadn't brought up the topic. There were some things too private to discuss with anyone, apparently. And there was so much to the interplay between her and Zach, subtleties she could never explain.

A small wail from the nursery relieved some of TJ's tension. She would hug Tina for the interruption, and she'd be careful to avoid this same conversation in the future.

Doreen stood up as TJ started from the room. "May I come with you?"

"Of course."

Doreen watched and cooed while TJ diapered and refreshed Tina. "She's so beautiful, TJ. She makes me want another baby."

With TJ carrying a fussing Tina, the women went to the kitchen. TJ quickly heated some formula and prepared a bottle. The baby took it greedily, as though she were starving.

They returned to the living room, where TJ sat in the rocking chair and Doreen remained standing. "I'd better get home. TJ, about Zachary..."

TJ raised her eyes from the baby. "I overreacted today. He surprised me, I suppose."

"He's a good guy. I don't think you should be afraid of his attentions."

"You're probably right. I'm not eager to get involved with any man right now, though."

"You had a rough time of it. Explain that to Zachary. I'm willing to bet he'll understand and not try to push you into anything you're not ready for. You will be, you know. Eventually you'll want another relationship. Don't close the door on Zachary."

Doreen started for the archway. "By the way, how long does he plan to stay with the company?"

"Another few months, maybe three or four."

Doreen nodded approvingly. "Good. By then you'll have everything worked out. See you soon. I'll let myself out."

"Thanks, Doreen. Drop in again."

When she and Tina were alone, TJ sighed and put her head back against the rocker. The baby was already getting sleepy again. Her normal schedule was off by a good two hours. TJ could only hope it would right itself naturally. Even little things like this demanded more of her time. How could she go back to work and pretend not to be concerned with every tiny nuance of Tina's care? How did other women do it?

This was serenity, joy. Nothing else even came close to the utter bliss of holding her baby and slowly rocking her while she drowsily consumed her dinner.

If only Zach had left things the way they were. She had been happier since Tina's birth than she'd ever been in her life. Now her peace of mind was cluttered with uncertainties, and with feelings she wished she had never experienced. She didn't need sex in her life, and that's what Zach had introduced her to today.

And now there were three problems to worry about: Zach's possible deception, her nearly obsessive drive to maintain the status quo, and sex.

TJ sighed again. How had she gotten herself into such a pickle?

Eight

Zach was watching the framers at the Hanson project. The four model homes were well underway. Rising from their concrete slabs like racks of dry bones, the ribs of the houses were rapidly taking shape. The air was turbulent with the noise of power saws, nailing guns, blaring radios and men's voices.

Construction crews were not quiet by nature, nor were they tidy. Boards, nails and debris were left wherever dropped. Normally each man participated in only one phase of the building process, and the cleanup people weren't given one dram of consideration from the framers, the electricians, the plumbers or the roofers.

For the most part, the men got along. They teased, joked and laughed while they worked, their banter adding to the noise of the scene.

But they didn't waste much time. Today's crew was moving fast, Zach noted, satisfied with the framers' progress.

He hung around for a few hours, then got into his rig and drove to the office. No one was there, which he'd expected.

Some of the construction crews consistently worked on Saturdays, but the clerical people only came in when absolutely necessary.

He settled down at his desk to go over his schedule on the Hanson project. Right after framing would come the air-conditioning people, then the electricians, the plumbers, the insulators, and so on. House construction was a very simple process, actually, a matter of one, two, three and on up to about a dozen steps. Each step had to be approved by a building inspector. A special card was kept on the site, and a builder could only proceed with the next step when the last one was signed off.

Zach sat back in his chair with a disgruntled expression. He didn't have to go over the schedule at all. He knew it as well as he knew his own name. He was as restless as a hungry cat, and he didn't have to wonder why. TJ's attitude was eating at him. She liked him, he knew she did, but she was dead set against anything personal between them.

And he kept coming back to the only reason that made any sense: He was an employee, *her* employee. As far as assets went, his were pretty slim these days. His savings account was growing, but he lived in a rented apartment with someone else's furniture. TJ's house was beautiful and any fool could see that she wasn't hurting financially. Zach didn't like thinking of her as focused on who had what in the money game, but he didn't know what else to think.

He wasn't always going to be an employee, as he'd told her several times now. But getting back on his feet economically was taking on new meaning. And it wasn't because he wanted to impress anyone, TJ included, with materiality.

But he didn't feel equal to her, and that gut-wrenching feeling was one that he'd never before encountered. He'd taken a lot of hard knocks in the past year. If anyone was shallow enough to think that what he'd lived through had been easy, they had another thought coming. He'd fought against believing Vincent's duplicity until it had been impossible to believe otherwise. Then the staggering shock of bankruptcy had hit him, when everything he'd owned had been seized to pay back taxes and past-due bank loans. He'd had as much or more as TJ did, and it had all melted away, like so much snow under a hot desert sun.

During it all, the pain, the shocks and the outright heart-break, he'd never felt as blue as he did today. He couldn't even seem to make a simple decision, whether to give TJ a report on the Hanson project by telephone or go to her house and present it in person.

TJ checked the chicken baking in the oven. She'd had company off and on for most of the day, neighbors, friends, everyone merely wanting to say hello and to take a peek at Tina. TJ had welcomed her guests enthusiastically. She'd worried her and Zach's situation to death and was tired of picking it apart.

Sad to say, the only solution she'd come up with was out-and-out candor, which she knew she wasn't going to risk. Not yet. In another few weeks, maybe. But right now she wasn't ready to take the chance that Zach would get mad and quit his job. A man's temper was unpredictable. Tommy's had been, she remembered only too well.

No, she was going to keep everything bottled up and pray that Zach wouldn't press her too hard on a personal level. If he did...?

Every time TJ reached that point, she shut down her thoughts. The image of making love with Zach was too disturbing to linger on. It awakened flickering fingers of response in her body but also fears in her mind, and thinking rationally, she didn't see herself needing either condition.

The chicken was doing fine and would be finished in about an hour. There was a mushroom sauce simmering on a back burner, and she would cook some wild rice and steam some broccoli. It would be a good dinner, even if she would be eating it alone.

By four she'd decided—with relief—that Zach wasn't going to drop by today. He hadn't called, either, but that was probably for the best, too. The framers would have stopped working by midafternoon, she knew, and Zach had probably gone home. He put in very long hours, nearly seven days out of every week. He was, without a doubt, the most conscientious employee she'd ever known.

Of course, TJ amended, it wasn't a given that Zach would have just gone to his apartment for the balance of the day. He must have friends outside of the company, both male and female.

The thought of Zach with a woman was like a sudden blow to TJ, and it staggered her to realize that she hadn't put him in that picture before. How incredible . . . and how remiss of her! A man like Zach would have women lined up at his door! They'd practically been lined up at Tommy's, and he'd been married!

Covering her face with her hands, TJ let a small groan escape from her tight throat. She was jealous and she had no right to be. What's more, she didn't want jealousy in her system! Not because of Zach, not because of anyone. She'd had enough of that with Tommy. Jealousy bred its own unique brand of misery, the waiting, the internal, eternal questioning, the pain, the never knowing what to expect or when to expect it.

No, she absolutely would not get caught in that trap again, not ever!

The doorbell rang at quarter of five. Wiping her hands on a towel as she went, TJ left the kitchen and hurried to the front door. Zach was standing there, which she'd suspected the second she'd heard the bell.

"Hello," she said calmly, a tone that belied the turmoil she was enduring. He looked freshly shaved and showered, wearing dark blue slacks and a paler blue shirt. He was shiny clean and blatantly male, and TJ's throat suddenly felt as though she hadn't swallowed anything except cotton for days. Her "Come in" sounded rusty, the result of an uneasy realization: If she consistently had these sort of reactions to contend with around Zach, something very odd was going on with her.

Zach uttered a quiet thanks and stepped inside. TJ looked like a frazzled-around-the-edges dream. Nothing could really mar that special beauty he always saw in her, but her green eyes had a harried expression. She was wearing a dress with a colorful floral design and a pink apron. In her hand was a small towel. Obviously she'd just come from the kitchen.

"I'm cooking," she told him.

"Sorry to interrupt."

"It's all right. Let me turn things down. Can I get you something to drink?"

She wasn't looking directly at him, an avoidance he couldn't possibly miss. "Nothing, thanks. I just stopped by for a minute."

They were still in the foyer, as though he hadn't been here dozens of times and wasn't used to making himself at home. Everything was different today. The strain in the air had them both uncomfortable.

TJ privately cursed her awkwardness. She had to lighten up. Treating Zach like a stranger wasn't going to alleviate their tension.

"Come on," she said with forced brightness. "We can talk in the kitchen."

"Fine." He stayed two steps behind TJ during the short trek through the house. Was this the way it was going to be between them from now on? With stilted conversation and uneasy glances? His stomach was tied in knots, and he'd bet anything that hers was, too.

In the kitchen TJ switched off two burners on the stove and then the oven. Zach saw the pots and the oven light. Good smells floated in the air.

He pretended not to notice and got right to business. "The framers made good progress today. We're right on schedule."

"Great." TJ fluttered from stove to sink and laid down the towel. "The air-conditioning people will get started when?" Untying the sash of her apron, she folded it and put it onto the counter next to the towel.

"Thursday morning."

"Well, everything is chugging along right on schedule, isn't it?" He'd already said that, but TJ wasn't thinking very clearly.

Zach was, though, and he didn't like what was happening. "TJ, would you rather I stayed away? I could keep you informed by telephone, if you prefer."

It was a challenge to the very foundation of their relationship. TJ's mind spun, with every aspect of her predicament vying for dominance. She couldn't insist on distance, not without risking his disfavor and her present freedom.

But he surely wouldn't suggest less interaction if he had plans to romance her into dangerous waters with the company. How would he gain anything in that respect unless she signed it over to him, anyway?

Was he completely innocent of the horrible suspicions badgering her?

Zach saw tears glistening on her eyelashes. "What's wrong?" he asked softly.

"Nothing," she declared huskily, and turned away to wipe her eyes. She felt him come up behind her.

"You're crying, TJ, and no one cries over nothing. I'm causing it, aren't I? Do you want an apology for yesterday? Would that make you feel better?"

"I . . . I'm all mixed up."

Zach put his hands on her shoulders and was glad when she didn't elude the contact. He hated seeing her so unhappy. He'd do almost anything to put a smile back on her face. "TJ, would you like me to find you another superintendent?"

"Oh, my Lord," she whispered, and squeezed her eyes tightly closed. She was so inept, so clumsy. Instead of reassuring Zach of his immeasurable value, she was giving him ideas about leaving.

TJ twisted around to face him. "That's the last thing I would like," she stated in a raw, hoarse voice. "Please don't even *think* about another super! You're the best, and you're the man I want."

The words hung in the air—*you're the man I want.* Their deep, immutable truth hit TJ hard. Her commonsense side might prefer otherwise, but as a woman, she *did* want Zach. The thought of him out of her life was horrendous, the thought of him with other women, stupefying.

"TJ..."

Such a wealth of feelings in a simple utterance! TJ's heart began a hasty beat from the sound, and from the expression on Zach's face.

There was moisture under her eyes, but her lips were suddenly dry. She dampened them and saw his gaze follow the movement of her tongue. In the next instant, they were in each other's arms, clinging together.

"TJ... TJ..."

"Oh, Zach..."

Their kisses were unaimed and hungry, falling on lips, cheeks and throats. Their bodies molded together, creating heat, and then shifted in an almost frantic search for further intimacy.

She felt the erratic movement of his hands on her dress, but her own hands were equally flighty. His heat seared her fingertips as she explored his chest and shoulders and throat. It was impossible to think clearly, so she quit trying after one small effort. Thinking had only been getting her in trouble, anyway, making her weepy and suspicious and not a very nice person.

Zach caught the back of her head. Their gazes met in a long, intense look that contained speculation and too many questions to count. One by one, as they continued to probe the other's eyes, the questions flicked away until nothing of resistance remained.

And then, with a guttural sound, Zach fitted his lips to hers. TJ's entire system seemed to explode. His mouth felt like nothing she'd ever experienced before. Except for yesterday's kisses, which had given her a stingingly strong hint of the depth of her own sensuality, something she'd never had tremendous faith in.

TJ knew she was reeling. Her knees had become some sort of rubbery substance, practically useless. Zach moved quickly and swung her up into his arms. She'd never been carried before, and the sensation was dizzying. Her dazed mind surveyed the kitchen. Dinner would be ruined. Half-cooked rice didn't survive a prolonged soaking. The broccoli would be green mush. The chicken would end up crisp in the slow-cooling oven.

In the bedroom hallway, Zach hesitated. "Which room?"

"Mine," she whispered.

He still hesitated. He'd visualized TJ in that pretty room, even in her bed, but now he was also seeing the shadowy ghost of Tommy.

"My room," TJ repeated softly. "It's all right, Zach. It's been completely redecorated with all new furniture since..."

Relieved, Zach nodded and headed for the master bedroom. When he was standing next to the bed, he let TJ's feet slowly slide to the floor.

"Before we...get involved, I want to check on Tina," she said unsteadily.

Zach nodded again. There was a very important third person in the house, and whatever he and TJ got caught up in, neither of them could forget Tina.

The baby's room was directly across the hall. TJ marveled that her rubbery legs brought her even that short distance. Her heart was like a jackhammer in her chest. Breathing calmly was impossible. She stood beside Tina's crib and looked down at her sleeping child with so much love, tears filled her eyes.

This was insane. Zach was in her bedroom waiting for her, and she was going to return and make love with him. It was so final, seemingly out of her hands. Why? How?

The answers that flitted through her mind were neither complete nor satisfactory. This wasn't like her. She was a woman who had questioned her own capacity for passion. There'd been moments when she'd even wondered about frigidity.

She wasn't wondering now; frigid women didn't quiver at a man's touch.

Sighing, TJ silently moved to the nursery door. Positioning it just so, she crossed the hall and then did the same with her own door. Zach was watching her, she saw, standing almost in the same spot where she'd left him. His hands were shoved into his pants pockets, and they appeared slowly as she walked over to him.

"Is Tina all right?"

"Sleeping like an angel."

Zach held up his arms and TJ stepped into them. She drew a deep, shaky breath as she laid her face against his shirt and wrapped her arms around his waist. He lowered his lips to her hair and kissed the top of her head. The ambiguities of her personality were present in her embrace, that same mixture of strength and vulnerability he'd noticed right from the first.

He wanted to reassure her, to tell her how important she'd become to him. His insides ached with more than just a desire to possess her body. Tenderness mingled with the demands of physical wanting, caring with the incredible sensations of holding her.

But he was afraid of too much honesty. With TJ he just didn't know. One minute he felt that he knew everything about her and the next instant he questioned.

He could show her how he felt, though, and maybe through lovemaking, he would know how she felt about him.

"Look at me," he whispered. When her head came up, his hands rose to her face and held it. His eyes were dark with pent-up passion. "You're beautiful, TJ, the most beautiful woman I've ever known."

She searched his eyes and stifled an urge to deny the flattery. She didn't believe him, not completely, but it was all right. People weren't really accountable for what they said at a time like this.

Rising on tiptoe, she brought her lips to within a fraction of his. His hands caressed her face and then moved slowly downward, following the contours of her throat, her shoulders, on down her arms to her hands, where he laced their fingers together.

Everything was in slow-motion. The urgency they'd exhibited in the kitchen had apparently been defused. They were going to make love and they both knew it, and their need for haste had evolved into a seduction of the senses.

TJ could scarcely breathe. She'd never been wooed like this. His mouth teased hers while his hands held hers at their sides. His teeth gripped her bottom lip for a heated second, the tip of his tongue slid across her mouth for another. Her pulse seemed in tune with the slowly ticking clock on the bed stand. Her blood had become sluggish, its pressure thick and throbbing in her ears.

And then, just as slowly, he began to undress her. TJ watched his eyes while he undid the three tiny buttons at the scooped neckline of her dress. He kissed the pulse beat at the base of her throat and then the tops of her breasts, still with that exquisitely leisurely pace. As though they had all the time in the world. As though the world outside of this house didn't even exist.

Maybe it didn't, TJ thought dizzily. Maybe this kind of sensation, this sort of intense pleasure, precluded all else.

She sighed, a soughing breath of utter mystification. It seemed that she understood herself very little lately, not since Zachary Torelli had walked into her office, to be precise. She looked at him queerly, and he smiled at her, a big, masculine smile that nearly buckled her knees.

He was good-looking enough to melt the coldest heart, and right now no portion of her anatomy was even slightly chilled. She lifted trembling hands to his face and moved closer to his body. She had never been aggressive with the opposite sex, but she was a different woman now than she'd once been. The changes in herself were becoming more apparent with each passing day.

He kissed her . . . or she kissed him. TJ didn't know who had kissed whom. But they were kissing passionately, and the urgency they'd left in the kitchen was back. His body rocked against hers, his hands were everywhere and his mouth was open and hot on her lips.

His thigh moved in between hers, and he lifted her outer leg, bringing it up so that his was pressed against her most secret and private spot. It felt incredible to her, sexy and naughty and thrilling enough to elicit a moan from deep in her throat.

His hand was under her skirt, she realized next. And it felt incredible, too, caressing her bottom, her thigh. Her skin tingled in the wake of its journey, and she wriggled against it, sighing huskily from the utter wantonness of their foreplay.

Her glazed eyes opened to see him looking at her. With their gazes locked and their lips parted for gasped breaths of air, Zach slipped his hand down into the band of her panties. She stared up at him and somehow made the decision that she, too, must explore.

She was about to follow through. Her hands had reached his belt. But then his fingers were between her legs, and she couldn't do anything but stand there and attempt to withstand the flames rippling through her body.

Zach saw what was happening and moved them both to the bed. They tumbled onto it, TJ on her back, him leaning over her. He pulled her panties down and opened her thighs. His mouth settled on hers while he picked up the rhythm he'd started a moment ago. It was good for her, he knew. Very good. She couldn't lie still, and her tongue was hot and greedy in his mouth.

It was the only way for a man to make love to a woman he cared about, see to her pleasure first. And there wasn't even the slightest question in his mind about caring for TJ. He more than cared for her, he was mad for her, desiring her in every way possible.

He stopped himself from pouring it all out. He wasn't going to scare her off at this stage, not when she was soft and pliant and aroused to tears.

He kissed the damp streaks on her cheeks, murmuring sweet nothings. His own body was aroused to the point of pain. After yesterday's frustration, it was a wonder he was able to maintain any control at all.

Her head moved back and forth on the bed. Perspiration had broken out on her temples, her upper lip, and her legs had bent at the knees and then sagged apart. She was open for him, ready, and he couldn't wait any longer.

He shed his shoes, socks, pants and briefs in record time. TJ's expression was dazed, he saw, as he quickly took care of protection. Her skirt was bunched around her hips, and she didn't even seem to be aware of the suggestive position of her body.

He looked at her female glory, her woman's secrets. She was beautiful...and waiting for him. He moved between her thighs.

TJ crushed him to herself. She was on the very edge, on the brink of something she had only touched upon in the past. Her system didn't seem to belong to her, driven as it was by inner forces. The weight of Zach's body felt uniquely male; that much was familiar.

The rest of it didn't seem real, her own heavy breathing, the heat and pulsating demands of her own flesh.

She gasped at the penetration she felt, and instantly the waves began. The spasms. The extraordinary, mind-bending pleasure. She cried out as it swept through her, again and again, engulfing her in ever-widening circles.

Reality began to creep in, Zach's movements, his low, guttural sounds. His back was dewy under her hands. His face was beside hers. She could feel his breath, and she closed her eyes and raised her hips to his strong, sure thrusts.

It was a ride to the stars, pleasurable every step of the way. She cried out again when he did.

They lay entwined for several minutes. TJ was stunned and unable to elude the feeling. Questions bombarded her mind, and finding no answers within herself, she resorted to tears.

Zach lifted his head. "What's this?" he asked gently.

"I . . . I've never . . . that was the first time . . ."

Surprise narrowed his eyes. "Never?"

She gave her head a shake, then shut her eyes in embarrassment. How could she tell him such a thing? Had she no pride whatsoever?

"TJ . . . let's get married."

Her eyes jerked open. "What?"

There was satisfaction on his face, an emotional contentment she'd never witnessed on his features before; there was pride and passion and promises; and there was a small smile on his lips and incredible warmth in his eyes. "It would be great for us, TJ. I've thought about it before. This isn't just an impulse."

Speech eluded her, but words scattered in her mind like straw before a gale, words and ideas stirred up by a tremendous dose of disbelief. Had she thought he would go this far? Was this his idea of a moving marriage proposal?

She would give him one benefit of the doubt ragging her: He was alone, and the idea of a ready-made family probably looked good to him.

But would she look good enough for a marriage proposal—offhanded as it had been—if she didn't own a successful construction company?

Nine

___

Every fear, worry, concern and niggling doubt that had been draining TJ returned in a confusing rush. Coming right on top of the most astounding physical experience of her life, the torrent was barely tolerable. Her heart thudded uncontrollably, her palms felt sticky.

"TJ?"

He was looking at her, she saw, dissecting her reaction. His expression was peculiar, questioning. She knew she had to say something.

She made a small throat-clearing sound. "Zach..." The right words were eluding her. She had to refuse his proposal, of course. It was ludicrous that he might suppose she would take it seriously. She had judged him as much more sensitive than this, which was another blow.

"Is it really so shocking?" he asked softly.

She tried to smile. "You...constantly surprise me."

"You surprise me, too."

TJ flushed. He was referring to her embarrassing confession. How could she have blurted out such a thing? Was it anyone else's business that making love had never been so good for her before?

She noticed his rumpled shirt then, and her dress. They hadn't even undressed completely. They'd been so eager, so impatient, going at each other with an almost savage intensity, her as much as him. The responsibility had to be equally shared. She must remember that. Except for that unexpected and horribly discomfiting suggestion of marriage, she was as much to blame as Zach for the situation.

Red-faced, TJ reached down and tried to cover herself with the twisted folds of her skirt. Zach's eyes darkened as he took her hand and stopped her rather frantic effort. He uttered one word, "Don't."

Her eyes lifted to his. He was leaning on an elbow, staring down at her. His voice was low, simmering with suppressed emotion. "Tell me what you're thinking."

The demand careened through her brain, knocking against truths, doubts and fears. How could she explain the convolution of her thoughts? There wasn't one completely clear idea anywhere within her, no acutely lucid statement just waiting to be said.

"Tell me, TJ, whatever it is."

She remained silent, her eyes fretfully darting from his and then back again.

"You can't tell me?"

"I'm not sure I know."

"You wouldn't be on this bed if you didn't have some feelings for me."

"Of course not."

"We're good together."

"I can't dispute that."

"But you can't talk about something permanent. That's it, isn't it? Hearing that I'm serious upsets you."

She was upset, all right. How could he think she wouldn't be? He hadn't even hinted at love, which was maybe only honest and to be appreciated. At least he wasn't a liar.

The hollow in TJ's midsection just kept getting bigger. Zach conveyed an air of waiting, as though it were her turn to talk and she had to have something important to say.

And she had nothing to say—not even a resounding "No!"

Zach watched her for another few moments with a disconsolate expression, then slid off the bed and picked up his clothes. TJ's gaze followed him as he walked into the bathroom. Did he understand how truly shocked she was? Was he thinking better of his astounding presentation: *Let's get married, TJ*. It was possible that he was as shocked as she was, now that a few minutes had diminished emotion.

She honestly didn't know what to think. TJ lay there for a moment, then covered her face with her hands in a wave of abject misery. Burrowing beneath the blankets and just plain hiding was appallingly appealing.

Her sense of self-preservation was especially strong with Zach. If he'd decided to romance her to get his hands on her business, he wouldn't be the first man to pull such a stunt on a woman. It was all so convenient for him, a ready-made family and the perfect business for his personal career preference, all in one fell swoop.

Or in one very heavy session of lovemaking.

Sick at heart, TJ sat up and slowly scooted to the edge of the bed. She would use the second bathroom to refresh herself.

When TJ came out of the bathroom, she went immediately to the nursery to check on Tina. The door was open much wider than she'd left it. She stopped. Zach was standing near the crib, gazing down at the sleeping infant.

Sensing TJ's presence, he turned. His mouth opened to say something and TJ put a finger to her lips. He nodded and looked at Tina again. TJ quietly moved to the crib. Tina would be waking up soon. She was still a little off her normal schedule, but hunger would be disrupting her sleep at any time now.

TJ's heart swelled with love as she looked at her precious daughter. The one emotional constant in her life was her love for her baby. The feeling was pure and beautiful and influenced by nothing else, the very first unconditional love TJ had ever experienced.

She glanced at Zach and felt a quick, sharp stab of awareness. His expression was as soft and adoring as what was in her heart . . . and he was looking at Tina, not at her.

She had recognized his affection for the baby before. He'd cooed and talked to Tina in as silly a manner as most adults did with an infant. He'd even asked to hold Tina, and TJ had carefully placed the tiny girl in his arms. He'd seemed in awe of the warm bundle of life in his hands and had talked about miracles, TJ remembered now.

The memory was jarring, and TJ motioned for them to leave with a tilt of her head toward the door. Zach responded with another nod, and the two of them tiptoed from the room. In the hall, TJ veered to the right, totally ignoring the master bedroom. Zach followed to the living room.

"I love her, you know," he said quietly.

TJ swallowed the sudden lump in her throat. Whatever game he might be playing with her, she didn't doubt that he had special feelings for Tina.

"So where do we go from here, TJ?"

She cleared her throat. "I don't want an affair."

His eyes flashed angrily. "I seem to recall mentioning marriage!"

"Yes, you mentioned it," she replied cautiously, succeeding with pronounced effort in keeping every trace of cynicism or sarcasm out of her voice.

Zach held out his hands, a placating gesture. "If you tell me to get out of your life, that's what I'll do. Not happily, I don't mind admitting, but if you don't want me around, I'll leave you alone."

TJ felt a scream welling within her. This was exactly what she had feared would happen. Her mind darted back to those trying months of operating the company without a reliable super, and ahead to how much more difficult long hours and the burden of responsibility would be with Tina constantly in her thoughts.

She felt the intensity of Zach's gaze and heard that same tension in his voice. "You really don't want me to stay away, do you?"

It was over, TJ thought with sudden weariness. There was a lot here she didn't understand, but she couldn't suppress her multitude of strange worries behind evasion any longer. Whatever came of it, going back to work full-time or not, it was time for some straight talk. "I'm not overly thrilled with the idea of marriage in general, Zach. I'm sure you know why, so let's skip past that unpleasantness. But putting you and I in that picture for the sake of conversation, as my husband, would you continue to work for the company? Would you be content to go on doing what you've been doing?"

Zach frowned. "You know my plans." The comment was made rather absently. His interest had been extremely piqued by TJ's remarks about her marriage. *Unpleasantness?*

"To own your own company again."

"That's my goal, yes."

"How about owning *my* company. Would you like to be a partner in Reese Home Builders?"

"Well, sure, but..." Comprehension was suddenly hitting Zach from every direction. Was *that* TJ's problem? Good Lord, did she really think he was after her company?

His mention of marriage *had* been impulsive even though he'd told TJ otherwise. He hadn't talked about love, because in all of the emotions TJ aroused in him, there were some he wasn't sure of. And TJ's on-again, off-again attitude toward something personal between the two of them hadn't exactly inspired confidence.

Still, this was something he couldn't have imagined in his worst nightmare. Had she been harboring this unholy suspicion all along or was it a brand-new notion? Where had it come from? Had he caused it without realizing he was doing so?

And then the agony of shock and disbelief began evolving into the whirling eddy of rage and outrage. "You think I made love to you to worm my way into your company?"

She hadn't expected such fury, but she recognized it. Oh, yes, Zach's expression of outrage was exactly the same one she'd seen on Tommy's face when she'd gotten too close to the truth of his misbehavior! She'd startled Zach with her perception and he'd reacted with defensive anger. She had been right. Her ugly suspicions had been right on the money!

Zach's mouth twisted. "If that was my motive, what was yours?"

"I beg your pardon?"

"You know what I said. You cooperated, TJ, as much as any woman I've ever known. More, maybe. You were hot for me, baby, steaming. Since we're discussing motives, what was yours?"

"You don't have to be crude."

"I could get a hell of a lot cruder!"

"And don't shout! You'll wake up Tina."

Zach drew a long shaky breath. "Fine. I'll try to calm down, but you've got some tall explaining to do."

"*I've* got some explaining to do?"

"You better believe it, sweetheart! What did I ever do to make you think I wanted your damn company? I told you what my plans were right away. I needed a job to earn the money to accomplish those plans, and it never once occurred to me to use you to get anything, least of all your business!"

TJ's eyes were smarting and her stomach aching. If she was wrong, her accusation was almost criminal. But wasn't it better to be overly cautious than not at all? Wasn't it only prudent for a woman alone—a woman with a child, especially—to be watchful and questioning of the people around her?

Oh, God. It was an internal cry, heard only by TJ. This was the end, of course. Zach couldn't possibly continue working for her after this.

"Please go," she mumbled thickly. She desperately needed to be alone. Too much had happened. A part of her was still shocked by her stunning participation in the bedroom. It demanded thought, analysis, and arguing with Zach would accomplish nothing, anyway.

"Oh, I'm going, all right." Zach started for the door, but after a few steps he stopped with a bitter expression on his face. "You're different, TJ. You impressed the hell out of me right from the beginning. I thought you were the most courageous woman I'd ever met. You were pregnant and a widow. You were in full control of your own business and doing a terrific job. I felt honored to know you and grateful to be working for you.

"Now I hardly recognize that woman. You're wrong about me, and someday you're going to realize it. And by the way, I *don't* know anything about your 'unpleasant' marriage. Whenever the opportunity came up to pry into your background, I let it pass, figuring that you'd talk about it if you wanted me to know."

Zach took two steps toward the door and stopped again. "I've got someone in mind who might be interested in the superintendent's job. His name is Carl Oakland. I'll talk to him about it, so if you get a call from him, that's what it'll be about. But whether he takes it or not, I can't stay. I'll come by the office on Monday and turn in the cell phone."

He went quickly then, leaving TJ standing in the middle of her living room. An overwhelming numbness kept her frozen there for several minutes. As though from a vast distance, she heard the sound of Zach's car starting and driving away. The house was morosely silent, like the eerie aftermath of a violent storm.

And then, from the nursery, the distinct sounds of her daughter waking up brought life back to TJ's body. Tears streamed down her face as she went to tend Tina.

* * *

TJ received a telephone call from Carl Oakland that evening. Within a very few minutes she had a new superintendent. She put the phone down and told herself it was best. Regardless of everything else, she trusted Zach's judgment on this, and if he recommended Carl for the job, the man would no doubt be good.

But he wouldn't be a tall Italian with vivid blue eyes and a beautiful, heart-stirring smile.

TJ got up and switched off the television set, which she hadn't been watching anyway. She'd tried, just as she had tried to resurrect the food on the stove and eat dinner. She desperately wanted to behave normally. Brooding over the situation would be pointless. Nothing could change what had occurred today, certainly not wishing to God that she hadn't gotten so physically carried away.

That sort of mindless passion had never happened to her before. She wondered whether she would even have heard her own baby if Tina had awakened and cried. Every sense she possessed had been focused on the man in her arms. Every minute portion of her body had been Zach's to command.

Maybe what bothered TJ most was an insistent question: If she was capable of such uninhibited sexual response, why hadn't it happened before?

TJ chewed on a thumbnail. She was profoundly unhappy and she might as well face it. Lecturing herself on the benefits of adult behavior toward an irrevocable event was sensible but not very effective. But Zach had also asked her to marry him and she couldn't stop thinking about it. What's more, she already missed him, and lying to herself about it only created stress. Zach wouldn't be dropping in anymore. Or calling. When she visited the job sites, he wouldn't be a part of the activity.

Something very large and important was missing from her life.

And from Tina's . . .

Not that the infant would even know it. She accepted attention from any soft-spoken person. Loud voices alarmed her, which Zach had seemed to know instinctively. His cooings had always been sweet and very quiet. TJ could still see his big hands curled around the little bundle they were holding. There was something immutably sad about Tina growing up without a man's affection. It was different than a woman's, just as tender but steadier somehow.

It was one more confusing issue, TJ decided wearily. Another reason to rue the day.

Well, there was no longer a cause to worry that someone was plotting to infiltrate her defenses and her company. If she ever even saw Zach again, the meeting would be accidental.

Of course, she could be at the office on Monday when he returned her cell phone. Daisy would watch Tina. TJ's heart beat faster at the idea. She knew that she wanted to see Zach again, but to what end? What would they say to each other? Would he cut her cold? Could she act as though he were only another employee breaking ties? Could he?

Whatever it turned out to be, the prospect was exciting to TJ. She had to contact Daisy and arrange a more concentrated care program in any case. There was no avoiding spending more time at the office and on the job sites until Carl Oakland proved himself, and who knew after that?

It only made sense to begin her more stringent work regimen on the first day of the new week.

Doreen looked up from her desk as TJ walked in. "Well, hi!"

"Hi, yourself."

"You're here bright and early."

"Early, at least," TJ said with a brief laugh. "Doreen, would you and Jim come to my office for a few minutes? I have something to tell both of you."

"Sure. I'll get him."

TJ went on to her office. Her system felt charged up, nervously jumping around. She had taken pains with her appearance. Her skirt and jacket were a striking plum color, complemented by a plum-and-lilac blouse. Her mid-heel pumps and leather handbag were also plum. Her hair was swingy and shiny and she was wearing makeup.

She had told herself while dressing that pride was her only motivation. Looking her best gave a woman confidence, and she needed all the confidence she could muster for the anticipated meeting with Zach.

Still, here in her office TJ felt overdressed. Her working clothes were usually slanted for comfort, not style. This outfit and a few others in her closet were worn for business meetings with bankers or developers.

TJ dropped her handbag into a desk drawer with a sigh. She was behaving out of character again, which she seemed to be doing with disturbing regularity lately.

Doreen and Jim walked in. Each was carrying a file folder, which TJ had expected. Since Tina's birth the two efficient employees had been calling TJ at home to discuss matters of immediate urgency. Less crucial problems or decisions were saved until TJ made an appearance.

Everyone sat down, TJ behind her desk.

"You look great today," Doreen commented with a cheery smile.

"Thanks." TJ's gaze moved back and forth between Jim and Doreen. "I'll get right to it. Zach and I had a misunderstanding and he's leaving the company."

"What?" Doreen's smile instantly disappeared.

Jim shook his head sadly. "I hate losing him, TJ. He sure knows his way around the construction business."

"Yes," she agreed quietly. "He was kind enough to locate another man, a Carl Oakland. Carl had some things to take care of today, but he'll be on the job tomorrow morning."

Doreen, TJ saw, was looking at her with a frankly appraising expression. After the conversation they'd had about Zach on Friday evening, Doreen wasn't going to accept TJ's casual statement of a "misunderstanding" without further explanation.

"Does Zach have a better job or something?" Jim inquired.

"He intends to start his own company," TJ answered.

"Well, I guess you can't fault a man for having ambition," Jim commented.

TJ's blood chilled. Her own ambition had driven her to study like a demon for the state contractor's test. It was ambition that had built this company, hers and Tommy's combined. His had slacked off, but hers had soared.

Until this past year. After Tommy's death she had been more concerned with protecting the assets she already had than with progress or ambition.

She suddenly felt sick to her stomach. Her caution had gone to extremes. Judging Zach's ambition so harshly was hideous, unforgivable.

Jim was getting to his feet. "Doreen can go over her items first, TJ. I'll come back when she's through."

"Thanks, Jim," Doreen murmured.

The two women were silent until Jim's footsteps had died away. TJ spoke first. "I know what you're thinking."

"Am I wrong?"

"I made a bad mistake," TJ admitted dully.

"Oh, TJ," Doreen moaned.

"It seemed so plausible."

"You couldn't accept the fact that he really liked you. Why, TJ? You're an attractive, intelligent woman. Why wouldn't a man of Zach's caliber like you?"

"I don't know. I just don't know. It all seemed to fall into place. I couldn't put it out of my mind. Everything he said and did kept aggravating the idea."

"And now you know you were wrong."

TJ took a breath. "I know it's *possible* that I was wrong, yes."

"Tell Zach."

TJ shook her head grimly. "There's no going backward on this, Doreen. I hired Carl Oakland, remember?"

"Did Zach . . . well, how angry is he?"

"He was furious. Insulted. Hurt."

"Oh, TJ." Doreen sighed sorrowfully. "Did you say right out that you thought he was only after the company?"

"Practically. Close enough."

Doreen sat back weakly, then indicated the file folder on her lap. "Are you in any mood to talk about this?"

TJ tried to smile. "No, but it has to be done, doesn't it?"

Some time later TJ was alone in her office, with both Doreen and Jim back at their own desks. The building's sounds were normal. The telephone was ringing every few minutes and snatches of conversations reached TJ's ears, although she neither listened nor absorbed.

Pushing her chair back from the desk, TJ got up and went to the window. Her mood had steadily gone downhill since her arrival. Memories were haunting her; regret was weighting her down. She'd had no facts, no proof, nothing to go on but groundless suspicion. She'd behaved like a child afraid of someone snatching away a favorite toy.

She wasn't a child, but was she frightened? She hadn't thought so. She'd seen herself as strong and coping.

Now she saw herself as pitiable, foolish, judgmental.

And vain. God, why had she dressed up today of all days? Would an expensive, becoming outfit impress Zach after what she'd done to him?

Not likely.

Sighing dejectedly, TJ glanced back at her desk. There was a stack of work on it that she wouldn't get through in only one day. Tina's tiny image appeared in her mind and TJ closed her eyes in a wave of longing. She wanted to be home, taking care of her baby, feeding her, diapering her, loving her. Did every new mother go through this unnerving period of guilt, and jealousy that another woman was caring for her child?

The jealousy might dissipate as Tina grew and required less attention, but what about the guilt? Tina had been born to her, and shouldn't a responsible parent raise her own child?

How did Doreen and a million other working mothers handle it? TJ realized that she'd never discussed the subject with her friend and secretary, an oversight she would correct in the near future.

Right now everyone in the place had work to do, including her. TJ returned to her desk and reached for the telephone. Before she got started, she would call home and check on Tina.

Total concentration was impossible. TJ kept glancing up from her work to the open door of her office. She was not at her best today, despite her stylish clothes. Her insides kept doing uncomfortable things, like slipping and sliding every time the front door of the building opened and someone came in.

And then, quite suddenly, she saw Zach walking by. He didn't so much as glance into her domain. TJ tensed and strained to hear as he began talking to Doreen. Rising quietly, with her heart beating a mile a minute, TJ walked to the foyer and looked over to Doreen's nook.

Zach's back was to her, but TJ could make out the conversation.

"I'm really sorry to see this," Doreen was saying. She had the cell phone in one hand, the extra battery in the other.

"Can't be helped, but thanks."

TJ swallowed hard. Just seeing Zach and knowing it was probably for the last time was horrible. His jeans and white shirt fit superbly, as did all of his clothing. His good looks battered TJ's senses. She knew so much about his body now, but there were still mysteries to the tall, ruggedly male form standing across the hall. Their frantic lovemaking had cheated her in ways that would be insignificant if applied to repeat lovers. She would know what his bare chest looked and felt like, for one major point.

TJ's palms felt clammy. Zach affected her like no other man ever had. Even when she'd been nearly nine months pregnant, she'd known that he radiated some kind of magic.

"I'll go back and say goodbye to Jim," Zach told Doreen.

"I know he would appreciate it, Zachary."

Zach walked down the hall and Doreen's eyes met TJ's across the distance. Doreen started to get up and TJ shook her head, telling Doreen silently that now was not the time to convey the concern that was so apparent on her face.

Men's voices came from the back of the building. TJ stepped back through her doorway, hoping to gain composure in the privacy of her office. Her heart was pounding, but she had to try to speak to Zach, even if he rebuffed the attempt.

It seemed like an eternity before Zach's boot steps rang in the hall again. TJ waited while he stopped for another word with Doreen, and then he was just outside her door.

"Zach?"

He almost kept on going, TJ saw with her heart in her throat. But he finally turned and looked through the doorway at her. "Yes?"

His eyes were as cold as ice. TJ's courage nearly deserted her. Her lips felt numb as she stammered, "Could...we have...a few words?"

His expression became impatient. "I think we said it all."

"No...please..."

Zach's hesitation wasn't intended as any kind of vengeance. He had no desire to hurt TJ, but he also had no desire to endure another round of accusations. She looked beautiful, more dressed up than he'd ever seen her. He honestly hoped she hadn't done it for this meeting. It was obvious, however, that she'd been waiting for him to get here.

"All right," he said tersely.

"Please come in."

His assent was grudging. He saw no point to unnecessarily refreshing pain, and that's all a "few words" between them could possibly accomplish. TJ had meant so much to him, and now he didn't know what he felt for her. She was still sexually stimulating, that might never change. But she had cut him to the quick, and the wound could be slow in healing.

TJ closed the door, something she rarely did. She liked her office open to anyone who needed her. At this moment, though, she wasn't thinking of anyone else.

"I'd like to apologize," she said, hardly able to look at the hard light in his eyes.

Zach wasn't able to reply right away. An apology for something so devastating was small comfort, he was discovering. He'd known that TJ would figure out how wrong she'd been, but he hadn't anticipated it happening so soon.

And, petty or not, he wasn't ready to forgive her. Her betrayal was like the crowning blow to a solid year of blows. His reaction to it was colored by months of other reactions. He'd overlooked, ignored and forgiven so many sins, and he felt now as if his usual forbearance had all but vanished.

Maybe, in time, he would get back to normal. He hoped so.

Right now, though, he couldn't be anything but cool with TJ. He moved around her, being very careful to avoid contact, and put his hand on the doorknob. "Goodbye, TJ."

"But..." Her expression was stricken. "Zach, I apologized! I'm sorry! Doesn't that mean anything?"

"Today? Right this minute? No, TJ, it doesn't mean one damned thing."

The door opened and he walked away. TJ stood there with her mouth hanging open. She hadn't let herself dare hope for complete forgiveness, but she hadn't expected a wall of icy resistance, either. She'd thought they might talk about the situation. Not that he would ever come back to work for her. She knew better than to even think along those lines.

But he was gone, and without accepting her apology. She was stunned beyond words, beyond even tears.

Doreen appeared in the doorway. "That was short. Are you all right?"

"I'm..." TJ drew a ragged breath. "I'm fine." She wanted to lump all men together and condemn their stubbornness, but even with indignation cramping her interior, she couldn't line up Zach with anyone else.

Besides, this was all her own doing. She was the one who had muddied the waters, not him.

Why was that so clear now when it had been so elusive before?

Ten

It was nearly two in the morning. TJ switched on the pool lights, then curled up on a patio lounge. The night sky was clear, the air chilly. Shivering a little, TJ wrapped the bottom of her velour robe around her bare feet.

The aquamarine water in the pool shimmered and shone. TJ had discovered a fondness for looking at it while she endured middle-of-the-night restlessness. It had been happening often lately. A deep sleep would suddenly just stop and she would be wide-awake.

She knew that Zach was at the core of her bouts with insomnia. His image haunted her nighttime dreams and her daytime existence, intruding on routines, habits and thoughts. She kept remembering, and shrinking a little more each time she did, especially when she got near the moment that she had cut him to ribbons with accusations. The memory of her own behavior was a constant, disruptive ache, and unilateral regret offered very little relief.

Watching the play of light on the pool water night after night, TJ battled her own personal demons. There was so much about the past year to puzzle over. Glimpses of clarity darted within the fog of complex questions and then vanished again before their implications made sense. Something—the hint of an idea, a feeling—kept eluding close scrutiny. Only one point was painfully clear: Every dram of her disquietude was richly deserved.

Sometimes TJ looked longingly at the phone, but her courage kept abandoning her. Through Carl Oakland—who was doing well with the super's position—TJ had learned that Zach had started another company.

It didn't seem to matter. Even her own company didn't excite her anymore. She was putting in more hours again and enjoying them less than she'd ever thought possible. The worst possible scenario had happened for a person of her previous ambition: She was working only because she had to.

Her entire life had become lackluster. Other than tending Tina, daily routines were dull and often boring. Bidding a new project only meant additional security—and work—when, in the past, the long, involved task had always presented an arousing challenge.

But then, nothing aroused her these days, nothing except the memory of one extraordinary encounter on her bed. She never walked into her bedroom without thinking about it, and it was persistently present behind every other activity she tried to bury herself in.

She was living with an unignorable longing for Zach, and she actually prayed that he was going through some of the same trauma that was keeping her so keyed up and restless. If he wasn't, if he'd truly put her out of his mind, there wasn't a snowball's chance in Hades of the two of them ever reconciling.

And, as the calendar moved toward the holiday season, reconciliation was becoming all-important to TJ, *some* sort of understanding. Friendship, if nothing else. She had to at least try, she told herself again as she straightened out her cramped legs and teetered to her feet.

Tomorrow, for sure, she would pick up the phone and make that call. These sleepless nights were becoming unbearable.

The office was unusually quiet. Doreen had left to take care of some errands, and even the phone had stopped ringing.

TJ eyed the instrument on her desk with every hair standing on end. It wouldn't be easy. If Zach hung up on her, she would be crushed. If he was cold...? Contemplating the possibilities had a nightmarish quality.

But it had been a month. Zach wasn't the type of man to carry a grudge forever. Maybe he was as ready to forgive and forget as she was.

Slowly picking up the receiver, TJ gently pressed out the listed number of Zach's new company. It rang two times and then a youthful female voice sang out brightly. "West Valley Construction Company. How may I help you?"

TJ cleared her throat. "May I speak to Zach Torelli, please?"

"He's not in right now. May I take a message?"

TJ thought fast. "Uh...yes. Please tell him that TJ Reese called. He knows the number. Ask him to call back when he can. It's...quite important."

"Sure will."

TJ put the phone down with an unsteady hand. She should have known Zach wouldn't be in the office, but his absence just might have been opportune. A return call could mean a great deal, indicating that he wanted to speak to her, that he was glad she had taken the first step.

TJ sighed. She was grasping at straws. Zach might merely return the call out of professional courtesy. They were both in the same business, after all.

She could only wait and see what he chose to do.

Tina was precious that afternoon, gurgling and cooing and melting her mother's heart into a soggy, sentimental lump. When the phone rang, TJ was sitting beside the baby on the blanket she had spread over the carpet. Tina was kicking her legs and waving her arms, enjoying a good stretch in just her diaper and undershirt.

"Mama will be right back, sweetheart," TJ told her daughter. "The phone's right over there. See? You can watch me while I talk." She picked up the phone. "This is TJ."

"My receptionist said you called."

The breath in TJ's body suddenly deserted her in one big whoosh. "Yes," she croaked without air. "Can you hold on for a second?" Without waiting for an okay, TJ covered the mouthpiece with her hand and took several long gulps of much-needed oxygen.

"I'm back," she finally said. "Thanks for calling. I wasn't sure you would."

"Is Tina all right?"

"Why, yes, of course. She's here in the living room with me, as a matter of fact. Lying on a blanket on the floor."

"Good. I was afraid you'd called to tell me . . ."

"No, no, it's nothing like that. Tina's fine, I'm fine." He hadn't asked about her, TJ realized the moment she'd said it. Only Tina. He sounded cool and distant, but if she was going to be put off by a little sign of indifference, she shouldn't have called him in the first place. "How've you been?" she asked with forced cheeriness.

"Busy."

"Carl told me about your new company. Congratulations, Zach."

"Is that why you called, to deliver congratulations?"

"Not entirely," she replied with mounting caution. He sure wasn't beaming all over the place just because they were talking. TJ was fast losing hope. He probably hadn't missed her at all.

"TJ, let's set the record straight, okay? I should have accepted your apology. I'm sorry I didn't. That kind of rudeness accomplishes nothing, but...well, I'm not looking for anything further between us."

That was plain enough for even a dunce to understand. TJ's weakened knees made the nearby chair very attractive, and she gratefully sank down onto it. "You haven't forgiven me, have you?"

"Does it still hurt, you mean? Yeah, it still hurts. Is that what you wanted to hear?"

"No...I...I'm sorry. I shouldn't have bothered you. Goodbye, Zach." TJ put the phone down.

She felt numb and stared over at Tina without really seeing the baby. Then, much like a sleepwalker, TJ got up and moved to the blanket, sinking to her knees beside her daughter. "He's still angry," she said dully. "I really didn't think he would be."

Tina chortled and kicked her legs. TJ smiled at her daughter through a mist of tears. "Your mother has turned into an awful fool, little darling. And she's trying very hard to figure out where it all went wrong."

Zach stared broodingly at the phone. He shouldn't have been so hard on TJ. It felt wrong, nothing to be proud of. Maybe he should call her again and...

And say what? *TJ, I'm still not over it, but I shouldn't have been so abrupt.* No, that didn't feel right, either.

He thought of her much too often. That business about her "unpleasant" marriage, for one thing, wouldn't leave him be. But there were other aspects of the time he'd spent in TJ's employ bothering him, too. For one, he'd never conveyed confidence with TJ. Not on a personal level. Not like a man did who *really* wanted a woman and did everything he could to let her know how he felt.

That day on her bed, for example. What would have been wrong with saying, "TJ, I think I've been falling in love with you ever since our first meeting?" Instead, he'd skipped past feelings and blurted out some nonsense about getting married. Even if she hadn't been choking on suspicion about him and her business, why would TJ or any other woman even consider such a stupid marriage proposal?

Where TJ was concerned, he behaved like a wet-behind-the-ears kid. The two of them were wrong for each other, and that was that. He knew that he was bitter about it all but couldn't seem to alter his feelings. Maybe he'd just had to swallow too many hurts in the past year to accept one more without bitterness.

Attempting to push the whole unnerving episode from his mind, he opened the file folder on his desk. He was making headway in the construction business again, albeit at a snail's pace. His limited funds was the main reason, although regaining people's confidence was also taking time.

None of the trials of getting started again were unexpected, at least. Not like this thing with TJ. He'd made a decision about her, and he was having a hell of a time implementing it. Why couldn't he just put her behind him once and for all?

Zach got up and poured a cup of coffee from the pot Debbie had left for him. His office was two rooms in a small building on the west side of town. His receptionist was inexperienced and very young, all he could afford. Debbie was trying hard, though, and would probably turn into a reasonably good employee.

It was a seat-of-the-pants operation so far, a day-by-day hope that only stayed alive from intractable determination. The first year was crucial in any new business. Getting established took time, patience and money.

The money was coming in fitful spurts. Zach had been contracting remodeling jobs and wielding a hammer right along with his one hired carpenter. He was on to something much better now, though, a modest apartment complex that would launch the company into deeper waters. One successful project of that caliber would be a giant step forward, and Zach was doing everything he could to land the contract.

He'd been working evenings on his bid for a week now. He had only one shot at the contract. He knew that his price would be considered with probably half a dozen others. He had one advantage over more established companies at the present, he figured, lower overhead. That would change when he really got going, but his lowly economic situation was actually a plus in the bidding game.

Carrying the cup to his desk, Zach sat down with a small grunt. He *had* to forget about TJ and concentrate on this bid. A lot hinged on attaining that contract.

A week later TJ was just taking Tina out of her morning bath when the telephone rang. She quickly wrapped the baby in a soft towel, propped the warm, damp bundle on her hip and went to the bedroom extension. "Hello?"

"TJ? Doreen. Listen, Patty has the flu. At least I think it's the flu. I've got to take her to the doctor this morning. I'm sorry, kiddo."

Patty was Doreen's youngest, and a sick child was more urgent than anything else. TJ kissed the top of her own baby's head. "Please don't worry about it, Doreen."

"I'll try to get to the office later on."

"Stay home with Patty today."

"I appreciate that, TJ, but there's one thing on my agenda that can't be put off. The revised plans on Hanson's Sonora model have to be delivered to county planning by four this afternoon."

"I'll do it. It's been a while, but I'm sure I can still find the planning office."

"You hate driving downtown," Doreen reminded her.

"True, but I can do it if I have to. Don't give it a thought. Call me after Patty sees the doctor."

"I will. Talk to you later."

TJ hung up just as a suspect moisture trailed down her hip. "You're leaking, little darling," she laughed, and carted Tina back to the bathwater.

The office was hectic without Doreen. Everyone answered the telephones, but TJ took the majority of the calls. By two she was glad to gather up the Hanson plans and leave the confusion to Jim.

The weather was perfect now, with bright sunny days and chilly nights. Anytime a breeze infiltrated the valley, the air was smog-free and sparkling, and today was particularly beautiful. TJ drove along counting her blessings. She should be happy instead of feeling depressed so much of the time, she knew, but she couldn't keep Zach at bay no matter how diligently she tried.

Along with Zach bothering her, however, was the general direction of her life. Money was not a problem and wouldn't be as long as she kept the company operating and solvent.

But was that all she had to look forward to? There seemed to be a terribly big hole in her existence. She adored her baby, enjoyed her home and owned a thriving business. She was busy every day of every week, and TJ knew that she should only be thankful.

It was deeply disturbing to realize that she wasn't, and she couldn't help wondering if she wasn't daring fate by wanting too much.

But she'd been finding herself envying Doreen because she had Jack, which seemed like positive proof that a good income and staying busy weren't enough.

She'd been so close to the fire with Zach. To that mysterious splendor that inspired poets and artists. That's what seemed to be dancing on the horizon these days, just out of reach, taunting her into almost constant dissatisfaction.

Had she fallen in love with Zach? Really fallen in love? The forever, till-death-do-us-part kind of love? Was that why she couldn't forget him now?

TJ's mouth was suddenly dry. Her fingers tightened spasmodically on the steering wheel. Why hadn't that possibility occurred to her before? But aside from that obvious oversight, why *else* would she physically respond to a man in such an uncharacteristic fashion?

"Oh, damn," she whispered, shaken to her very soul. She didn't need this now, not when she knew with every certainty that Zach wanted no part of her. She'd had her chance with him, a very large and incredibly beautiful chance. Instead of nurturing it, she had destroyed it with a few horrible words. And to realize now that she was in love with no chance at all was stupefying.

The whole year had been traumatic, TJ thought glumly. Even before Tommy's death she had been profoundly unhappy. Not with the business. She'd never been resentful of the business until after Tina's birth. But nothing else had been right for a long time, which had no doubt contributed to her wariness with Zach.

It was all so senseless, so unnecessary in retrospect. The timing had been off. She hadn't been ready for a man like Zach. She'd been pregnant and self-protective when they met, and after Tina's birth, the protectiveness had gotten all out of proportion.

The thought of her working and living on one side of town and Zach on the other, of never seeing him again, on and on into a bleak and lonely future, brought tears to TJ's eyes. She had to blink very hard and fast to maintain clear vision, and she had to resort to trite phrases to keep from breaking down completely. *Things could be worse. Don't dwell on it. Life goes on.*

It was really the traffic that settled TJ's emotions. One couldn't drive a car in Las Vegas's congested downtown area without concentration. Tourists crowded Fremont Street, and only one block over on Carson Street, visitors to city and county government offices vied for parking space. TJ drove to the county building in which the planning department was located, finally found an empty slot in the parking lot and pulled into it.

Life *did* go on, and she had a business to run. Sighing, TJ gathered up the plans and her purse and got out of the car.

TJ was on her way out, having delivered the revised Hanson plans to the proper authorities for approval. Coming toward her in the long corridor was a group of well-dressed men. One of them stepped away from his companions. "TJ?"

"Hermie! How nice to see you." TJ hurried over to the middle-aged gentleman with her hand extended. Hermie Cohen clasped it warmly.

"How are you, TJ?"

"I'm fine, Hermie. I have a daughter now, you know. Tina is three months old."

"I'm happy for you, honey. A child is a wonderful gift. Are you still running the business?"

"Oh, yes," TJ concurred with a nod. "I'm surprised to see you here. Are you back in Vegas to stay?"

"I just completed a development in the San Diego area." Hermie smiled. "And yes, I'm back here to stay. Have you heard about the proposed Galaxy complex, by any chance?"

TJ laughed. "Everyone's heard about the Galaxy, Hermie. Are you involved?"

The dapper gentleman made a cutting motion at his own throat. "Right up to here, honey. I was planning to call you. I'd like to work with you again, and someone's got to be the primary contractor on the Galaxy. Think you'd be interested?"

TJ felt a quick rush of adrenaline. For the first time in months a project was exciting. The Galaxy had been discussed in the newspaper for a long time. It was to be a major development, incorporating a shopping center, condos and single-family dwellings. Much bigger than anything Reese Home Builders had ever tackled, it would require monumental expansion.

But the primary contractor would reap a fortune, and it seemed utterly incredible that Hermie Cohen was offering such a plum to her.

The pitfalls would be as staggering as the possible profits, TJ realized in a deflating wave of reality. Her face fell, which the keen-eyed developer didn't miss. He reached into his pocket for a business card.

"Think about it and call me in the morning," Hermie said gently. "The decision must be made without delay, TJ. Construction is slated to begin within six months, but you understand the complexity of preconstruction preparation."

"Yes," TJ said in a near whisper. This was the opportunity of a lifetime. But the question of whether she wanted such an opportunity was running wild in her brain. The work would consume every hour of every day for at least two years. Her present routines...with Tina...with the business as it was now...would be altered to the point of unrecognizability.

But Hermie Cohen didn't finance unsuccessful projects, and his vote of confidence was an honor she couldn't reject without some very serious consideration.

She straightened her shoulders. "Thank you, Hermie. I'll call you tomorrow morning with an answer."

After Hermie had returned to his friends, TJ slowly moved down the corridor to the building's main entrance. Only a year ago she would have been doing handsprings at the offer she'd just received; today it tied her in knots. Facing such an extensive project alone was almost beyond comprehension.

TJ went through a revolving door, barely noticing her surroundings. Lost in thought, she made her way to the parking area on instinct. She had to stop a moment to remember where she'd left her car, and when she looked around, her eyes widened in stunned surprise. Zach was three parking aisles over, just getting out of his Wagoneer.

He hadn't seen her, TJ realized. He looked marvelous, tall and straight and crisply handsome. Seeing him made all of her fanciful thoughts about having fallen in love suddenly crystal clear. She *was* in love with Zach Torelli, deeply, abidingly in love. Her spirit rose to a dizzying height. He had asked her to marry him, and what if she had said yes? Without that ghastly suspicion inhabiting her soul, she might have.

Regardless, Zach had to have felt something important for her to have even thought of marriage. It couldn't all have disappeared.

Hope and despair battled within TJ. This unexpected opportunity seemed crucial. Unless she did something obvious, Zach would never know they had been in the same place at the same time. He wasn't looking in her direction.

Opportunities were hitting her from unusual and diverse sources today, first Hermie's offer, and now this. Mysterious forces were at work—if she could just interpret their meaning. Hermie . . . Zach . . . the Galaxy . . .

And then, in one of those flashes of piercingly sharp clarity, everything fell into place. TJ stood there another moment. Her mind was racing, functioning, she knew, as it used to, with perspicacity and clean, uncluttered logic.

She drew a deep, unhurried breath and then began walking, intercepting Zach just as he cleared the end of the aisle he'd parked in.

"Hello, Zach."

His eyes snapped to her as he came to an abrupt stop. "Hello, TJ." His gaze traveled the length of her, absorbing cream-colored slacks and royal blue sweater, before halting on her face. There was an odd excitement lurking in her eyes, and if it was because of him . . . ?

Zach's own reactions weren't what he'd expected from an accidental meeting. It was just short of stunning to realize how glad he was to see TJ, but that's exactly what he felt.

He was staring and TJ knew she'd surprised him. She didn't want to give him time to remember his anger, so she plunged headlong into her plan. "I'm glad we ran into one another. I've got a business proposition to talk over with you. It's very good, and I'm positive you'll be interested."

"Business?" His tone was skeptical.

"*Strictly* business. Something very big and very exciting."

So the excitement in her pretty eyes wasn't for him, after all. The letdown in his gut wasn't very pleasant, Zach noticed, wondering what the hell was going on here. Where was the resentment he'd been living with? He'd had no trouble locating it when TJ called last week.

But then she'd only been a voice on the phone. Right now she was standing close enough to touch, and he was inhaling her scent, factors that were decidedly affecting his attitude.

"How about a cup of coffee?" TJ suggested brightly.

"Right now?"

"I've only got until tomorrow morning to make up my mind, Zach. It's a golden opportunity, believe me."

Zach's eyes narrowed. "But what's it got to do with me?"

"That's what we have to discuss."

She'd said "strictly business," which seemed utterly astounding for the two of them. After their little brouhaha, did she actually think they could do business together? And taking it one step further, if they *did* manage that enormous hurdle, did she really see their future relationship as only platonic?

Then again, he might be forgetting TJ's dedication to business. Maybe she wouldn't have a moment's trouble keeping things impersonal between them.

Damn, he was feeling it all again, the desire, the satisfaction and then the pain. Dealing with TJ wouldn't be at all good for his mental health.

"I don't know," he said thoughtfully. "Maybe I'd better pass."

"Zach, this project would establish you and your company like nothing else ever could. At least give me a few minutes to tell you about it. Please don't discard it because of…well, because of what I did. I understand how you feel about me on a personal level, but I think you approve of my business ethics. This really would be strictly business. Please believe that." TJ mentally crossed her fingers as she spoke. Everything she'd said was true expect for that "strictly business" hogwash.

Zach shifted his weight uncomfortably. It shook him that TJ could propose a business arrangement between them and look as cool as she could be about it. How could she, after all that had happened?

Still, he was in no position to deliberately ignore a "golden opportunity," was he?

"All right," he conceded. "I'll be free in about ten, fifteen minutes."

"We could meet somewhere. How about McGraw's? They serve great coffee, and it's not too far away."

"Fine. See you there."

He wasn't happy about this, TJ acknowledged as Zach strode away. But he would be. No budding contractor could possibly pass up an opportunity like the Galaxy. The project would put the two of them together again, and once that happened . . . ?

A frown appeared between TJ's eyes. This was about as devious as a person could get. She was deliberately planning to mislead Zach to convince him that her only goal was the Galaxy.

TJ watched his tall form winding through the parking lot and then raised her chin determinedly. She couldn't give up on Zach without a fight. If that made her a calculating female, so be it. But if there was the slimmest chance that he was in love with her, too, she wanted to find out.

Eleven

TJ had a pot of McGraw's specially blended coffee and a plate of bite-size shortbread cookies already on the table when Zach arrived. The place contained a smattering of other coffee drinkers, but he noticed that TJ had obtained a table well away from anyone else.

While he sat down, TJ politely filled his cup. They both took a taste, eyeing each other almost cautiously across the table while they sipped.

"Do you know Hermie Cohen?" TJ asked then, fitting her cup back onto its saucer.

"I've heard of him. Why?"

"He's the man behind the Galaxy complex, Zach."

Zach's entire person instantly radiated incredulity. "Are you and I here to talk about the Galaxy, by some wild stretch of the imagination?"

"Yes," TJ replied evenly, although she was tremendously pleased with Zach's excitement. "Hermie offered me the primary contractor's position today."

"You're serious?"

"Very. He asked me to call him in the morning with my decision."

Zach sat back with a long, drawn-out, "Phew!"

"To say the least."

"Well, *I'm* impressed. How about you?"

TJ picked up her cup and held it with both hands. "I can't do it alone."

"Cohen must think you can."

"Hermie's faith is flattering, but I know my own limitations. Let me put it this way, Zach. I don't even intend *trying* to do it alone. If you're not interested in getting involved, I'm going to refuse the offer."

"TJ, this is the kind of opportunity that every contractor dreams about!"

"I realize that, and there was a time when I would have stood on my head for a chance at the Galaxy. But things have changed. I'm not going to ignore Tina for two years, which is exactly what would happen if I undertook something of this size by myself."

Tina. Sweet baby scent and miniature fingers and toes. TJ hadn't been the only female haunting Zach. The stern lines of his face relaxed. "How is she, TJ?"

A smile broke out on TJ's lips. "Growing like you wouldn't believe. You should see her hair. It's getting thicker and so pretty. And her eyes are as blue as..." TJ's gaze mingled with Zach's "...as yours," she finished softly.

Zach felt a flush creeping up from his shirt collar. But before he could formulate a reply, TJ became all business again. "I'd like to form a partnership between our companies."

Zach gave a short laugh. "Mine's nothing to get excited about. I've been doing remodeling, TJ. Right now I've got a good chance of landing the contract for a thirty-six-unit apartment building, but I won't have a final answer on that for a few more days."

"It's not your company that's crucial to this decision, Zach, it's you. You're the best. It's as simple as that."

"You know as much about construction as I do."

TJ smiled. "Maybe. But I already told you why I won't take on the Galaxy project alone. So...the ball's in your court. What do you say? Are you interested?"

He'd never been more interested in anything in his life, except maybe in TJ herself. Apparently that was a thing of the past, though, a romantic little interlude that had caused nothing but trouble for both of them. TJ had put it behind herself, obviously, and he'd damn well better try harder to do the same. Passing up this opportunity would be idiotic when it was the very height of his career aspirations.

TJ was intent on Zach's reactions. Considering her lowly opinion of her own acting ability, she was doing a remarkable job of appearing calm.

This wasn't *all* deceit, she told herself. What she'd just told Zach was true. She would not tackle a massive project like the Galaxy complex on her own. Not these days. When Tina got older, maybe. Money just wasn't as important to her as it had once been.

While she gave Zach time to digest her offer, TJ thought about loving him. He was a proud, sweet man, and she could see how hard he was attempting to conceal an elation he simply could not conquer.

It felt good to admit her feelings, to bask in them, even if she couldn't yet pass them on to Zach.

But they would be seeing each other again. A lovely sigh whispered through TJ as visions of private conferences and a rebirth of their previous close working relationship took shape in her mind.

Then a small chill skittered up her spine. Zach was thinking, she could tell, remembering. He wasn't over the pain she'd inflicted, and he was feeling it again.

Nervous suddenly, TJ reached for the pot and refilled their coffee cups.

He spoke, his voice cooler than it had been. "An extensive project like this would be fertile ground for mistrust."

TJ's heart skipped a beat. She'd displayed critical mistrust before. Zach had a sound basis for bitterness and every right to bring up any and every infraction she may have committed. And it was occurring to her that, contrary to what she had sensed from him only a moment ago, he wasn't going to blindly dive into anything with her, not even for something as compelling and profitable as the Galaxy complex.

He was still hurt, still trying to deal with it. TJ recalled him saying during their final fiasco that she had some "tall explaining" to do. She had explained nothing, she realized now. But how could she have, when she hadn't understood herself until very recently?

She tried to speak matter-of-factly, as though this conversation wasn't one of the more important of her life. "An apology is only words, isn't it?" Zach's eyes conveyed agreement. "I've thought about that day so often," TJ continued quietly. "And about what led up to it. What caused it. It didn't just happen, you know. Spontaneously, I mean. What I said to you had been eating at me for quite a while."

"My God, why?" Zach questioned low and tensely.

"Some sort of personal insecurity," TJ said with a sigh. "I've torn it apart and that's the only thing that makes any sense. The odd thing was, I knew deep down that you weren't capable of such deception. And still the doubts broiled and festered. The whole year was traumatic and a period of transition, Zach. I probably didn't trust anyone."

"You trusted Doreen and Jim, which you well should have."

"Yes, that's true. But neither of them was a personal threat."

"And I was?"

"You were asking more of me than I was ready to give," TJ assented softly. The question of what stage she was at now hung in the air, but TJ didn't expand on the subject.

Zach stirred in his chair for a moment. "Maybe *I* should be doing a little apologizing. I never thought of it from that angle before."

"No more apologies, please. Insecurity doesn't excuse my behavior. I accused you without just cause, Zach. You had every right to anger."

Was he approaching a change of heart now because of the incredible business deal TJ had brought to him? The question stuck in Zach's craw, creating unease, discomfiture. He liked that they were talking, and TJ's logic seemed reasonable. He'd sensed her vulnerability right away, too, so her admitting insecurity now wasn't a cop-out.

Zach took a big swallow of his coffee, then set the cup down. Working together again was a possibility—not a certainty yet, but the potential was sitting right here at this little table with them.

He looked at TJ thoughtfully, a long enough stare that she squirmed. "What are you thinking?" she finally asked.

"I'm wondering if it would work."

TJ leaned forward with glowingly hopeful, eager eyes. "It would, Zach. What I'd like to do is call Hermie in the morning and set up an appointment for the two of you to meet."

"How do you know him?"

"Through the business. The company did several jobs for him in the past. He always praised our dedication to detail."

"Was he Tommy's contact . . . or yours?"

"Would it affect your decision if he'd been more Tommy's friend than mine?"

"Maybe, maybe not," Zach answered truthfully. "Right now I'm not sure of anything, but I am curious."

"I see," TJ said musingly. "Well, as it happened, I met Hermie first. A banker friend introduced us. The company was really just getting off the ground, and Hermie was involved in much smaller projects in those days. He progressed quickly, moving from residential to commercial developments within a few years. Then he went to California, which is where he's lived until now. Running into him today was pure chance, but he said that he'd been planning to call me."

"He knows about Tommy, of course."

"He came to the funeral, Zach."

Zach looked off across the coffeehouse. "I'm sorry. I'm not intentionally digging up the past, but I can't make this kind of decision without knowing a few facts."

TJ studied his profile—and the strained set of his shoulders—until he brought his gaze back to her. "What else would you like to know?" she asked.

Zach hesitated. He had to know about her "unpleasant" marriage, even though it probably had nothing to do with what was going on now. "About you and Tommy," he said in a low voice. "Can you talk about it?"

TJ drew a long breath. Other than with Doreen, she had never really discussed her marriage with anyone. Oh, some of her neighbors and friends had hinted for information, and she hadn't been able to sidestep them all. There'd been brief conversations about the accident and occasional vague references to Tommy's life-style, but she'd never started at the beginning and told the entire story to anyone before.

And that's what Zach was requesting.

All sorts of thoughts flashed through TJ's mind, about trust and honesty and her own natural reticence. About how naked she would be if her private life were no longer private. But Zach wanting to know and asking was elating. Wasn't candor the first major concession in an important relationship?

A flush of excitement warmed TJ. Aside from her personal hopes for the two of them, she truly wanted Zach to have the Galaxy. The project would put him at the top of the heap in the construction community, which was where she truly believed he deserved to be. But she knew Hermie, and he wouldn't award a job of this scope to someone he hadn't done business with before. He would, however, accept Zach's participation if she requested it.

TJ prepared herself for a much longer meeting than she'd anticipated. They had a lot to talk about and she was extremely pleased at the progress they were making. It was remarkable that they were talking at all, and she would do almost anything to sustain and encourage what was developing between them again. She glanced at her watch. "I'm due home, Zach. I need to call Daisy."

Zach got to his feet as TJ rose. "Don't let me interfere with your schedule."

"Please, you're not interfering with anything. I'll only be a minute."

McGraw's had a pay phone in its foyer, and while TJ headed in that direction, Zach slowly sat down again. Her partnership offer roiled and mingled with his personal feelings. He sipped coffee and tried to separate the two, discovering very quickly that he couldn't do it. Working together would fan every emotion he'd ever felt for TJ back to life. Just seeing her, talking to her, was already doing it.

And yet, the Galaxy deal would secure his company's future. It was a hell of a problem.

Not for TJ, apparently.

A period of trauma and transition was what she'd labeled the past year, which was understandable. Anyone undergoing the shock she had would need time to get over it. Apparently he'd rushed her, which he hadn't meant to do. There'd been so much going on between them, exchanged looks, warmth, a wealth of unspoken but shared responses.

Or so he'd thought. He'd been mistaken, obviously. She hadn't been ready for another man, and he'd pushed her into making love with him.

Would he do it again? If they spent the time together that the Galaxy project would demand, would he have the strength to withstand his intense attraction for TJ, or would he, at some point, make another pass?

"Damn," he muttered under his breath. TJ set his hair on end and pretending otherwise would be utterly senseless. Didn't she have any instinct about such a relationship? Hadn't it crossed her mind what countless hours and days and *months* together could cause?

But then, she had called last week, hadn't she? And from what she'd said today, she'd had no previous hint of the

Galaxy project entering her life. So, did her call mean she had hoped for some sort of reconciliation?

He was really in the dark with TJ, Zach admitted uneasily. When he'd tried to forge a stronger bond between them, she had literally turned on him. Now, today, she seemed businesslike and yet more open, more like the woman he'd fallen so hard for.

TJ returned before Zach had unearthed any brilliant solution to the complex situation. She looked a little breathless, a tad anxious.

"Zach," she said as she slid onto her chair. "I talked to Daisy. I'm terribly sorry, but she has dinner plans and can't stay with Tina past five. I was thinking. If you wouldn't mind potluck, we could continue this discussion over dinner at my house. The decision on the Galaxy *has* to be made tonight, and I don't think you're quite ready to give me an answer. Maybe with a little more conversation . . ."

Zach held up his hand. "Slow down, TJ. You're running faster than an overwound clock. Give me a minute, okay?" He needed more than a minute—more like a week—but he didn't have a week. It seemed a little odd that Hermie Cohen would suddenly drop such a choice job on a contractor, but Zach had been around enough to know that unexpected things did happen in business.

Zach looked at his own watch, then back to TJ. "It's four-thirty. You're going to have to get going."

"Yes. I've been putting in shorter days than I used to. Daisy is accustomed to my getting home around four."

Dinner at TJ's loomed as a dangerous beginning to a long-term working relationship. She was too pretty and fired too many memories to risk an intimate evening in her home.

But then, he might be the only one who would even notice. She seemed to want the Galaxy deal but was reluctant to take it on alone. He wanted it, too, and was leery of the partnership. They were single-minded on the business aspect of the offer and miles apart on the personal.

She was right about one thing: This conversation was far from over.

Zach pushed his chair back. "I'll follow you home."

TJ breathed a sigh of relief. "Great."

Daisy passed the baby to her mother, chatted a moment and left. Zach stood around until the congenial older woman had gone, then advanced on TJ and Tina. He couldn't believe how much the little one had changed in five, six weeks. He touched her tiny hand and watched it curl around his forefinger.

And then she gurgled and smiled at him. Zach stared at the phenomenon as though he'd never before seen a smile. "Hey, look at that. She likes me. Do you remember me, sweetheart?"

"She has a tooth," TJ said proudly. "Can you see it?"

Zach bent lower and peered into Tina's rosebud mouth. "It looks like a little piece of rice."

TJ laughed. "Yes, doesn't it? It's a tooth, though."

It took an hour to feed Tina her dinner and get her ready for bed. Zach watched the process with a feeling of awe. Tina was the first infant he'd known from birth, and every movement and sound she made seemed to be nothing short of miraculous. She was so much more alert than she'd been the last time he'd seen her, and she kept looking at him with her big blue eyes, melting his heart a little more each time she did it.

"She's a happy baby," TJ told him with her pride showing again. "Her pediatrician told me that some babies cry a lot. Tina never has. Only when she's hungry or uncomfortable."

"Maybe she's happy because she's got such a good mother," Zach said quietly.

TJ sighed. "I don't know about that, Zach. Daisy spends more time with her than I do these days."

"Which bothers you."

"Look at her, Zach," TJ said softly. "She's so tiny and helpless. Yes, it bothers me to leave her with someone else. It bothers me a great deal."

"But Daisy is conscientious, isn't she?" Zach asked with some alarm.

TJ couldn't help laughing. "Daisy is wonderful. I don't have the slightest complaint about the quality of Tina's care. That's not the point."

Zach's eyes narrowed on mother and child. Despite that note of laughter, TJ was deadly serious about this subject. She didn't like leaving Tina with anyone else, regardless of how wonderful the person was.

The Galaxy offer was beginning to make more sense. TJ had mentioned in McGraw's about not wanting to neglect Tina for two years, and he'd accepted the explanation without really grasping it.

Now he grasped it fully. TJ didn't want to refuse Hermie Cohen's offer, but she would, rather than face the time-consuming project without a dependable partner. Out of all the people she knew, she'd chosen him, which was indisputable proof of trust.

Belief struck Zach in resounding waves, belief that TJ truly regretted her unfounded accusation. In a flash of total enlightenment, he realized that until this very moment he'd been doubting her apologies. He'd been harboring the hurt she'd perpetuated, almost protecting it.

Something gave way within him. He'd taken out an awful lot of resentment on TJ. Yes, she'd struck without warning, but he'd overplayed his role in that sad chapter of their relationship.

"I'm going to take Tina to her room," TJ whispered. "She's getting sleepy."

The little one's eyes were glazing over. Zach nodded silently, then on impulse, bent down and placed the gentlest of kisses on the baby's forehead. Her powdery scent and delicate skin jolted through his system, a feeling like none he'd ever experienced before. Love for a child, an infant, was like no other love, he admitted as TJ smiled warmly at him, then quietly left the living room with Tina in her arms.

Zach plopped down in the nearest chair. He wasn't accustomed to rubbery knees and a soft, sinking sensation in his gut. His gaze slowly swept TJ's attractive living room. He maybe shouldn't be feeling as if he'd come home, but TJ and Tina and, yes, this house, meant more to him than anything else in the world.

With his elbow on the arm of the chair, Zach dejectedly leaned his forehead into his own palm. How could he work with TJ feeling the way he did about her? Sure as shootin', he'd blurt it out at some inopportune time, and what would she do or say the next time he brought up feelings she didn't want to hear about?

She had two important elements in her life: Tina and the company. Could he remember that indefinitely? For two years, at least? He'd thought—*hoped*—that he had locked TJ in the past, along with Vincent and Vista's bankruptcy and every other painful segment of the long year.

TJ wasn't going to stay invisible, though. She was going to keep him reminded, in one way or another, of the overwhelming mistake he'd made with her. He'd assumed too much, concluding erroneously that affection was a two-way street. He'd learned the hard way that it wasn't. One person could really care about another, while the recipient of that affection remained only a casual participant.

Zach looked at the demise of his original company as a harsh lesson learned; he wouldn't make the same mistakes with his present company. He had to use that same principle with his and TJ's relationship, he realized now. The Galaxy was too good to pass up. But he had to keep his feelings for TJ to himself.

He vowed on the spot to keep his hands off TJ and his mouth shut, no matter how tempted he might become to do otherwise. He'd been slapped down enough. She wanted to work together. Fine. The association would benefit both of them. He needed her—she needed him. They would make money and progress in the business world. The partnership she had suggested made good sense.

But that's where their interaction would stop. As she'd said so distinctly, this deal would be strictly business.

A snarl of loneliness and rootlessness hit Zach then. There was a hell of a lot more to living than making money and progress in business. TJ, at least, had Tina. He had no one, which was his own fault. Since TJ, he hadn't even asked a woman out to dinner.

That would have to change. He'd have to at least try to muster up some interest in other women. Someone would come alone with the ability to replace a small blond lady with big gray green eyes in his heart. All he had to do was open his mind and his eyes. The world was full of attractive women.

TJ, minus Tina, stuck her head in. "I'm going to see about dinner, Zach."

"Fine." Zach got up and tracked TJ to the kitchen, putting his avowal into practice by forcing himself to ignore the arousing shape of her behind in those tailored slacks. Oh, he'd been noticing, all right. Noticing too damned much. That blue sweater, for one thing, had a knitted design that revealed without overly hugging her figure. And he'd been aware of the way her hair swung with her movements, and the glow of her skin, and the unique color of her eyes. Details that he would have to concentrate on disregarding.

"Don't go to any fuss for me. I'm not very hungry," he said stonily. It was true, he wasn't a bit hungry. Too much had happened that afternoon and food just didn't have much appeal.

"You're not?" TJ stopped with her hand on the refrigerator door handle. He didn't look very happy, she realized uneasily, letting her hand slowly fall to her side. "How about something light... an omelet, maybe?"

"Anything." Zach perched on one of the tall stools at the counter. "If you want some help, let me know."

"No help needed, thanks." Something rather serious had altered Zach's mood, TJ sensed, and it had happened during the few minutes she'd been in the nursery. She felt his eyes following her as she got eggs, cheese and milk out of the refrigerator. A slow burn began inside of her, an awareness

of blue, blue eyes and a long, lean body draped over the
stool and countertop.

Could she work with this man at close range for an indefinite period of time without giving away her feelings for
him?

Her hands weren't quite steady as she broke the eggs into
a bowl. "It's been a while since I've made an omelet," she
murmured, wishing she could breathe a little more normally. This was awful. If she couldn't control her reactions
any better than this, she'd scare Zach off.

"Talk to me about your marriage," Zach said quietly but
firmly. He still wanted to know. Even with nothing but
business in his and TJ's future, he had to know about her
"unpleasant" marriage.

TJ cast him a quick glance. He wasn't playing any kind
of game, she saw from the serious expression on his face.
He'd wanted to know about Tommy in McGraw's, and he'd
apparently waited as long as he could to remind her of it.

She nodded. "Yes, all right." Just thinking about the
years with Tommy brought a cacophony of emotions. So
much had happened and she'd been so dreadfully hurt.
That's what Zach wanted to know, wasn't it? It was her own
reference to unpleasantness that had made him so curious,
after all.

But instead of words about the painful old memories that
were suddenly crowding her soul, TJ heard herself saying,
"Tommy wasn't happy. He needed a different kind of life
than we had, a different kind of woman than I was. Than I
am. He looked for something else, which ended up making
us both unhappy."

Zach recalled his one meeting with Tommy Reese and
tried to sharpen the indistinct recollection of the woman on
his arm. She hadn't been TJ, that's all he knew for sure. The
overall picture was becoming uncomfortably clear: Tommy
had had a roving eye.

"There was someone with him in that accident," Zach
said very gently. "I wondered if it was you."

"Me?" TJ sent him a sharp glance, then began to beat the eggs. "No, it wasn't me." The mixture in the bowl was quickly turning to pale yellow froth, but she kept on beating it. "She was Tommy's most current . . . friend, I guess."

"But she wasn't hurt?"

"Only enough to demand a large settlement from our insurance company. I don't know if she got it or not. I never asked. According to the police report, her blood alcohol level was off the chart, which weakened her claim of innocent victim. That's really all I know about her. It was a one-car accident, thank God. They were near the California state line in the middle of the night and the car rolled."

Talking about it was tough for TJ, Zach could see. She was punishing the eggs and appeared unaware of it. He shouldn't be putting her through this. Why was her past life so important anyway? What possible gain was there in dredging up old hurts?

He got off the stool and walked over to her. Regardless of his oath to keep things cool between them, he couldn't stand seeing her unhappy. Especially when he'd caused it.

Without warning, TJ just seemed to wilt. Placing her hands on the edge of the counter, her head dropped forward. Zach clasped her shoulders from behind. "Take it easy, honey," he soothed softly.

Her hair concealed her face. "I found out I was pregnant a few weeks later. It was my doing. We had grown so far apart. I worried constantly. I wanted Tommy to face what was happening to us, and I . . ."

"Don't," Zach whispered. "I understand."

His nearness was seeping into TJ's ragged emotions. She could feel his warmth at her back, the strength in his hands on her shoulders. Love for him swelled within her, eclipsing old sorrows and painful memories. A sob welled and escaped, and she clamped her lips together to preclude another.

"Turn around, honey," Zach said gently.

She pivoted slowly with her heart in her throat. This was the Zach she had fallen in love with, the caring, kind, hopeful man who had walked into her office with a section of newspaper that memorable afternoon. She'd never given falling in love at first sight much credence, but it was a distinct possibility with her and Zach. Certainly it had happened within the first few weeks of their relationship. And oh, how she'd fought it.

She was all through fighting the best part of herself. Besides, right now she couldn't fight anything, not even the tears spilling from her eyes. She'd had no idea how emotionally devastating talking about Tommy to Zach would be.

Zach wiped away the telltale moisture beneath her eyes. "I made you feel bad. I'm sorry."

"It...had to be said," she said in a near whisper. "I thought you knew all about Tommy. So many people do. And you said you had met him."

"Only once. I barely remember the incident."

There was a shadowy fire in Zach's eyes, and TJ stared at the flickering emotion with a quickening pulse rate. They were standing so close to each other, mere inches apart. And he didn't seem to be thinking about widening the gap.

Nor was he thinking about the Galaxy.

TJ took an anxious breath. If he made even the slightest move toward her, she would fling herself into his arms. And if that should happen, she would tell him how much she loved him.

But he wasn't going to make that move, was he? TJ blinked as comprehension slammed her mind. Zach might offer compassion and comfort by drying her tears, but that's all he was going to do. It was a shock for TJ, because she sensed so much more from him. There was desire in his eyes and in his stance, but he wasn't going to do anything about it!

She dampened her lips. If she touched him, would he back away?

Zach's eyes narrowed slightly, and TJ suspected that he understood what was going through her mind. It was up to her, she realized. This was her chance to express her feelings. He'd taken the risk once and she had crushed him. He could very well be hoping for the opportunity to return the wound.

Or he could be merely leery of another such disaster.

Her legs felt like two limp carrots. Why, in every emotional crisis, did her legs turn feeble on her? She could look for support from the counter behind her... or from Zach.

She hadn't planned this. The Lord knew exactly what had gone through her mind in that parking lot, and she hadn't hoped for this sort of emotionally charged moment so soon. Hermie's offer had provided a heaven-sent opportunity to spend time with Zach, and that's all she had envisioned for the two of them for a long time to come.

But she couldn't let this moment pass. They were on the same wavelength right now, and it might not ever happen again. It wouldn't, she suspected, if she set the tone of their future relationship by ignoring the present challenge.

Gathering her courage and praying he wouldn't be offended, TJ took the tiniest of steps forward and laid a trembling hand on Zach's chest.

Twelve

The warmth of the hand on his chest rocketed through Zach's system with tremendous impact. What was TJ doing? He reacted with a sharply drawn intake of air. After the vow he'd just taken, there was something ironic in her making this kind of move.

But he didn't really know what kind of move this was, did he? What did she want from him? What did she expect him to do right now?

She was a total enigma, and while he'd never once thought of TJ as ditzy or scatterbrained before, he was beginning to wonder. Who was she testing with that hand on his shirt, him or herself?

Zach knew only one thing. He wasn't going to help her out in this. Whatever was in her mind—and it was more than the Galaxy project—he wasn't going to make it easy for her. Maybe he'd uncover, once and for all, just what it was she *did* want from him.

TJ still wasn't sure that he wouldn't back away, maybe get angry with her. This was bold of her, very brash, very nervy.

Her heart was pounding furiously, but she was driven to push on and see what happened. Her hand made a tentative movement. Zach's shirt felt soft, the muscles beneath it a stunning contrast. His heartbeat pulsed in rhythm with her own, coursing through her fingertips and up her arm.

His eyes were narrowed on her face, and she read a dare in them. Something rebellious in her nature arose and accepted the challenge. She brought her other hand up and put it on his shoulder; the contact felt achingly exquisite.

Her hands slowly roamed, absorbing the planes and contours of his chest and shoulders, his upper arms. "I wondered about this...after we..."

His eyes darkened. "I rushed you that day."

Her smile contained feminine mystique, which Zach didn't miss. "We rushed each other."

Ah, yes, he was getting the message. This had every possibility of ending up in the bedroom, and TJ making the first move was utterly amazing.

The Galaxy venture was probably as real as rain, but this was TJ's true motivation in bringing them together again. Now all he had to do was figure out why. She'd balked at the idea of an affair—which hadn't been his goal, either—but that attitude might have changed. She'd been damned changeable in everything else.

Zach gritted his teeth. It was taking superhuman effort to stand there without grabbing the beautiful, ripe woman tormenting him. His mind took off, devising images to fit what his body was demanding. He saw himself snatching away her clothes and unzipping his jeans.

He gave his head a quick, sharp shake. This was TJ's game, and he wasn't going to either help or hinder her, not if it killed him.

It wasn't going to kill him, although the pleasure was as close to agony as anything could get. He couldn't control two things, his breathing and what was happening in his jeans. But he kept his hands at his sides while she slowly undid the first button at the top of his shirt.

TJ had never felt such power before. This beautiful, sexy man was trembling because she was touching him! He might not be helping, but neither was he protesting. It was astounding, exhilarating. With his shirt open, she pressed her lips to the sprinkling of black hair on his chest. Then her tongue found a pebble-hard nipple and licked it.

Zach groaned and closed his eyes. His hands had formed fists, but they were still down by his thighs.

"Am I...bothering you?" she whispered. It was an inane, flirty question. Of course she was "bothering" him. She was also "bothering" herself. But she'd missed him so terribly much, and somehow she had to rectify the ghastly mistakes she'd made.

"You know damned well what you're doing to me."

"Do you want me to stop?"

"TJ..."

He'd sounded desperate. She tipped her head back to see his face. "Tell me what you want."

Forgetting his decision to leave this encounter entirely up to her, he lifted a hand to the back of her head, tangling his fingers in her hair. His eyes were murky with emotion. "What do *you* want?"

"Haven't I made it obvious enough?"

"Sex? Another roll around your bed?"

She flushed. "More than that."

"Love, TJ? Something permanent? Are we talking commitment here?"

She forced herself to look directly into his eyes, although her longtime protective shield was urging retreat. Zach couldn't be really cruel if he tried, she honestly believed, but there was a harsh sort of ruthlessness in his expression. He wasn't going to accept evasion.

TJ's chin lifted a fraction. "I...love you." It wasn't a strongly stated, full-of-confidence confession, but it was all she could give. Courage with a man wasn't one of her strong suits, she had discovered. If Zach gave her any encouragement now, her next words would have more substance.

Zach drew a ragged breath. Her hands were in his shirt, his in her hair and on her back. TJ had the power to wring him out. He didn't feel instant elation at her almost timidly spoken declaration. The words whirled around in his brain, creating questions instead of peace.

But then, he was so torn up, maybe only one thing would calm him. Maybe, like apologies, admissions of affection were merely words. Maybe *making* love was the only way to settle ragged, ruffled emotions.

TJ's heart seemed to have gone mad in her chest, pounding with trepidation and outright panic. She'd just confessed a very private feeling and Zach wasn't responding! He'd heard, he understood, but he wasn't responding!

And yet she sensed his physical response to her nearness. There was no mistaking the heat in his eyes, no misinterpreting the message of his hands, one of which moved in her hair and the other on her back. The hard, fast thudding of his heart beneath her own fingers was more evidence, and most of all, the very air they were both breathing was alive with emotional turbulence.

Words weren't enough, she realized then. She would have to show this proud man the depth of her feelings for him. His own feelings were locked and guarded, and could she fault his reluctance to free them? Hadn't she been doing very much the same thing until recently? In fact, she hadn't even faced the word "love" until today. Why? What was so frightening about love that a person would dance around any recognition of it until it simply rose up and refused denial in such blatant terms, one could no longer ignore its presence?

TJ knew the answer to that heartrending question but put it on simmer for now. She would think about it later. Right now there was something much more urgent to attend to.

Dampening her lips while she rose to tiptoe, she leaned into Zach and brought her mouth to within a fraction of his. "I want to make love with you," she said huskily.

It was what he wanted, too, so badly, in fact, he was in misery. His entire nervous system jumped when her hand slowly slid down his chest, and he closed his eyes to savor the intoxicating pleasure of the caress she administered to the front of his jeans.

"You want to make love, too," she whispered.

He hesitated, then wondered why, when his arousal was so evident. He no longer felt resentment toward TJ. She'd reacted to circumstances, the same as he had.

But this was all her show. She was the aggressor this time, and he was going to milk it for all it was worth. If she really meant it, if she really loved him...? Lord, what if it was true? Why would she say such a thing if it wasn't?

Zach nearly lost control. Playing the passive role in love-making was totally foreign to him.

But there was also a compelling excitement about it, an erotic provocation he'd never before experienced.

It was as unique as TJ was, he thought with some wry-ness. Right from the beginning TJ had wrenched his emotions in unparalleled ways. There were just some things a man knew nothing about, simply because he hadn't met one particular woman.

Life was darned strange.

TJ was amazed at her own grit. Her own shamelessness, she amended quickly, for she felt absolutely no shame whatsoever in touching Zach so intimately. She loved doing it and kept on doing it while she pressed her mouth to his.

A low growl rumbled in his chest. His lips moved with hers, and the big hand in her hair flexed and gripped her scalp tighter. The kiss was heady for TJ, fogging her brain. Desire swarmed in her body like a hive of buzzing bees.

Her hand on his fly was driving him up the wall. They both had too many clothes on, and Zach wondered dizzily how she would get them from here to her bedroom. He could easily take over right now. He wouldn't have a bit of trouble getting them down the hall and to her bed.

It wasn't a matter of risking more heartache with TJ any-more, but male pride and stubbornness refused to assist in his own seduction. That's what she was so engrossed in, and probably what she'd had in mind all along, right from the moment she'd asked for a few minutes of his time to discuss a business proposition.

She wasn't thinking about business right now, he knew. But then, neither was he. She was breathing in small gasps. Her breasts were pushed into his chest, her lips tantalizing his, her hand moving on his fly.

Her tongue slid into his mouth and his knees nearly buckled. He couldn't take any more. If she wanted to play, he'd play. Maybe they'd talk later, maybe not. Right at the moment, with every nerve in his body jangling, finishing what she'd started was the only thing in his mind.

He scooped her up into a hard, fierce embrace, lifting her clean off the floor. Startled, TJ's arms quickly locked around his neck. "Zach..."

His mouth on hers prevented further speech. There was very little gentleness in his lips. He was rough and impatient, hot and excited. Zach ordinarily thought of himself as a pretty easygoing guy, but he'd been pushed to the maximum limit during the past year. It hadn't all be TJ's doing, and to think otherwise would be unfair.

But she'd done some pushing, all right, and she was in his arms. So was every minute they'd shared, their own mind-boggling session of lovemaking, her accusations, her apologies, her partnership offer today.

He wasn't himself right now, Zach knew, and he still couldn't beat back the frustration and anger that seemed to have taken control of his senses. They had been simmering, apparently, camouflaged by a veneer of civilized behavior, but now the emotions that had been building for months were escaping like compressed steam through a tiny crack in a boiler.

TJ felt the change in him. His arms were hard around her, his breath coming fast. Zach felt driven, and he had no experience with such a tremendous inner force. He kissed her again, his body burning from the heat of his own emotions. His mouth possessed without consideration. His tongue thrust into her mouth without gentleness. He was on fire and she had caused it. She had kindled and teased it to life, and she was going to extinguish it.

Some tiny seedlings of regret sprouted in TJ. What had she done? This man was not the Zach she knew and loved. This man, with his hard, rough arms and lashing mouth was a stranger!

She pushed against him, her palms on his shoulders. Her shoes were nearly a foot off the floor, dangling somewhere around his knees. His arousal ground into her thighs. He was hot and hard and incredibly strong. He could do anything and everything to her that should enter his mind.

Tears stung her eyes. Would he tear off her clothes? Lay her down right here on the kitchen floor?

Her pulse began to beat faster. *Tear off her clothes?* Two could play that game. She wasn't really frightened, she realized, not a bit. She'd done everything but stand on her head to seduce him—which honestly hadn't been part of her plan back at the county parking lot—but success with her own endeavor was nothing to be leery of.

Yes, he was inordinately worked up. But no more than she was. Throwing caution to the winds, TJ grabbed the two panels of his shirt at his throat and yanked them apart. A button gave somewhere, she felt it pop. Zach felt it, too, and raised his head to stare at her with a puzzled expression.

His mouth glistened with moisture and looked swollen and sexy. TJ leaned forward and ran the tip of her tongue over it. "Do you like it rough, darling?" she whispered. "Is that what you want?" She nipped at his bottom lip. "Are you going to tear off my clothes?"

He swallowed. "Don't tease anymore. I've had about all of that I can take."

"Who's teasing?"

His almost hostile gaze probed hers. His passion had given up some of its ragged edge, but he had to have her very soon now. He hurt bad and could barely breathe. She might not be teasing, but neither was he.

As for wanting it rough, he only wanted it, right this minute any way he could get it.

Whirling, he started for TJ's bedroom. A glance at her face surprised him: She was wearing a completely female, smugly satisfied smile. This was exactly what she wanted from him, what she'd wanted all along. His lip curled cynically. Why had he looked for some big, secretive reason for her behavior? It was so simple. She'd liked sex with him and she wanted more. Sure she "loved" him. Most women "loved" a lover.

In her bedroom, Zach sat her on the bed and immediately straightened up to undress. He was strung out, he knew, but some sizzling lovemaking would take care of all that tension.

TJ watched him toss his shirt to a chair and then yank his white undershirt over his head. His naked chest was magnificent, more beautiful than she'd imagined. His belly was flat and tightly ridged. The bulge below his belt distorted the shape of his jeans, but the pants were quickly dispensed with, his undershorts, too.

Mesmerized, TJ sat there and stared. This was the pleasure she had missed the first time they had made love, the wonder of just looking at him. He moved closer, and impulsively she scurried across the bed to its other side. Getting to her feet, she began to undress.

He was watching her every movement with dark, stormy eyes. He was so unbelievably handsome he took her breath. He looked like a bronze sculpture of the perfect male with his dark skin and black hair.

Whisking away the sweater, TJ fumbled with the waistband of her slacks. Her bra was a creamy lace fabric, and Zach's gaze was fixed on it. Her skin tingled while she slid her slacks down, and then she was barely covered by lace in two areas.

Her eyes met his across the bed. Slowly she brought the straps of her bra down and reached behind herself and unhooked its clasp. The wispy garment fell away, and she saw Zach's chest heave with a mighty breath of air.

"I wasn't teasing you in the kitchen," she whispered huskily as she slithered the silky panties down her thighs.

"Weren't you?"

TJ caught the top of the spread and drew it to the foot of the bed. A blanket and sheet were quickly folded back, leaving an inviting nook of pillows and pale pink sheets. "I'm not teasing now, either," she said softly. "Come to bed with me."

She thought about saying it again: *Zach, I love you. Don't you believe me?* He was so intense. She'd worked him up to nearly savage desire, and herself, too. First they would make wild and wonderful love, and then maybe those magical words would just erupt on their own.

He reached for her the second they had both touched the sheets. His hands were greedy adventurers, traveling over her bare skin while his mouth claimed hers in a long, drugging kiss. When he needed air, he kissed her throat, her shoulders, her breasts.

But even the enticement of her soft breasts with their rosy, puckered nipples couldn't delay the inevitable for very long. He was on the edge, and he'd go over with or without her very soon now.

He moved into position, cradling himself in the vee of her thighs. An apology for his haste was on the tip of his tongue, but he couldn't seem to get it out.

Her lips parted when he penetrated her femininity. She was beautiful, glorious. Her eyes were dark green and enormous, staring up at him with so much adoration he froze for a moment to wonder about what he was seeing.

But then the moist heat of her body squeezing his eradicated that conjecture. He wouldn't last, he knew, not without a few tricks. The question was, did he want to simply take his own pleasure or make it good for her, too?

He rested on his forearms and watched her face while he moved very slowly, one of those "tricks" to maintain control. Her eyelashes drifted down and up, giving him glimpses into her soul. Her tongue wet her lips, and her hands moved on his shoulders.

"You like me making love to you, don't you?" he whispered.

"Yes."

"Is the Galaxy for real, or just a trumped-up reason to get me involved again?"

She brushed a lock of black hair back from his forehead. "It's for real."

Zach closed his eyes and let the pleasure flow. He didn't understand TJ and maybe never would. She loved him, so she'd said. They were sexually in tune, able to arouse each other to the point of near madness. And, last but probably as crucial as anything else, they were in the same business.

Maybe it would all work out. Maybe he was too damned sensitive about love and a solid future together. Unrealistic. The world functioned differently these days. Some people considered marriage old-fashioned.

Some people, not him.

What's more, he would have bet anything before he'd really gotten involved with TJ, that her values were very similar to his. The funny thing was, he hadn't recognized his own values until the past year.

There were lessons to be derived from even the most painful adversity, apparently.

Zach felt TJ's hands creeping up around his neck. He opened his eyes and saw how affected she was by his taking-it-easy brand of loving. For a few minutes in the kitchen, he could have torn off her clothes, just as she'd suggested. She wouldn't have minded, either. She was a sexy, sensual woman and unashamed of her passion for him.

He dipped his head and touched his lips to hers. "It's good slow, isn't it?"

"It's very good," she whispered.

"Makes a person a little crazy, hmm?"

"It's very...compelling." Emotions were battering TJ. So easily, too easily, she could spill out her feelings again. This time in detail. Distinctly, with no holds barred. She wasn't just making love, she was *in* love. But if neither of them ever even mentioned the word again, she would do everything she could to preserve the desire between them.

They *were* going to have a future together, and she would
not risk losing Zach again for any reason.

"TJ..."

Her heart nearly stopped. He was looking down at her
with the most loving expression she had ever seen on a man's
face.

"Yes?" she whispered, afraid to hope that he might say
the words that were in her own heart.

"TJ..." His hand rose to brush the slightly damp hair
back from her forehead. Avowals meant little at a time like
this. They were communicating on the most elemental level,
joined as only a man and a woman could be. He loved her
and wanted to say so.

But he stifled the urge with an agonized groan and forced
his thoughts into safer territory...to the here and now...to
the ecstasy of having her beneath him.

He began to move faster, with deeper plunges. No more
tricks, he thought. No more delays, no more fighting the
pressure. Vaguely he was aware that she was with him,
moaning hoarsely with each glorious thrust. Her pleasure
mattered to him, no matter how blasé he'd tried to be about
it. He knew so well how impossible it was to understand
TJ's passions. He'd thought he'd known her and he hadn't,
and it was a matter of learning acceptance now.

Her legs came up around his hips. She was writhing beneath him, feverishly participating. Her face was flushed
and dewy. Her fingernails were digging into his back.

And then she began to cry out, a low, keening sound that
sent Zach's senses flying into outer space. The ultimate thrill
was solely hers for several seconds, and then theirs, together, for several more. The shooting pleasure in his body
was so intense it was almost painful. He groaned out loud,
again and then again, and squeezed her so tightly, she
moaned.

He was drained, utterly exhausted, and he collapsed in a
wave of total fatigue. He wanted to sleep, to just close his
eyes and drift off into some faraway land of peace and se-

renity. He kissed TJ gently and moved to the bed, curling around her.

TJ couldn't speak, either. Reality returned slowly. The firm male body fitted around hers felt like a safe harbor, and gradually her thoughts began to take shape again. Her response to Zach was overwhelming, even more so than their first time together. Would it just keep getting better for them? She had heard of that sort of lovely communion, but had never imagined it happening to her.

Why had she been such a god-awful fool before? When Zach talked about marriage, why hadn't she thanked God and seen into her own heart? Why had it taken so long for her to recognize her feelings?

TJ's mind went back to the first day Zach had walked into her office. She'd seen him as special even then, and each day after that had reinforced her initial impression. They had become closer and closer, without putting anything into words, until that final weekend.

And then she had yanked the rug right out from under his feet, throwing him completely off balance. She'd turned on him at a particularly vulnerable moment, when he was open and trusting and talking. If she had encouraged instead of hindering, they might be at a vastly different stage now.

Tears filled TJ's eyes. Zach didn't know what to make of her, did he? She had confused him so badly, he was wary of exposing himself again. He wouldn't repeat that mistake, not with her, at least. She had to face it: Their future relationship would consist of working together and, to put it bluntly, sex. She'd said it plainly enough, I love you, Zach. And he hadn't acted upon the confession. Hadn't expanded its possibilities.

TJ lay there while the room gradually darkened. Tina could wake up and demand another bottle yet tonight, or she might sleep until early morning. She wasn't consistent in her evening routine anymore. She was growing, changing daily.

TJ closed her eyes in hopes of falling asleep, too. Zach was sleeping soundly, his right arm across her waist a dead weight.

She sighed softly. Being in bed with Zach felt strange. The whole day had been strange.

But something important had begun. Zach was back in her life. He would accept the Galaxy deal, of course, how could he not? And they would continue with their relationship as it was now until they were better able to discuss feelings. Someday...

TJ stiffened. What about Tina? Could a relationship based solely on sex do anything but harm her child? Right now Tina was too young to realize that a man was in Mommy's bed, but what about in a few years? Time sped by. What kind of questions would Tina ask in a few years?

TJ's heart started pounding. What, in God's name, had she been thinking? She'd been so concerned about leaving her baby in another woman's care, and now she was planning to do something that could ultimately bring Tina a lot more distress than a loving, thoughtful sitter. Was she mad? Was her passion for Zach destroying her good sense?

It could not go on and on and on into an indefinite future. Without children involved, adults could indulge themselves to their hearts' content. They could play their games and delay commitment until they were old and gray, and no one was hurt by their behavior except themselves.

A dark cloud of gloom had replaced TJ's previous contentment. Slipping from beneath Zach's arm, she carefully got out of bed. The room was dark, and she cautiously went to the closet for a robe. Tying its sash around her waist, TJ padded barefoot across the carpet to the door.

She silently moved to the nursery and switched on a small lamp. Tina had wriggled in her sleep. Her blanket was off, and TJ tenderly arranged the soft square of flannel over her daughter's tiny form.

Then she sat in the rocker and put her head back. She had to face things as they really were. Working with Zach again would be impossible without a repeat—*many* repeats—of what had happened this evening. They were lovers, and as long as they were anywhere near each other, that status would not change.

They were both stumbling over pride and self-protectiveness. They could make love, but they couldn't talk about love. They had both been terribly hurt in the past year, longer than that to be more accurate.

But understanding the past was no excuse for risking the future. Especially Tina's future.

TJ drew a long, slow breath. Her alternatives were limited. So were Zach's. They *had* to communicate. They had to swallow their pride and say what they really felt.

She had to spell it out to him, without evasion, without vacillation. They were in an all-or-nothing situation, and the sooner they decided which it was, the better off they'd be.

Sighing, TJ got to her feet and tiptoed back across the hall. She would let Zach sleep tonight, but first thing in the morning, she would initiate a very pivotal conversation.

Thirteen

Zach stirred with some uneasiness. The room was dark and he was coming awake to unfamiliar surroundings. The bed wasn't one he was used to. The sheets were silky soft and smelled clean and lightly perfumed.

Like TJ did.

That's where he was, he realized, in TJ's bed. Not alone, either, although he might as well be. She was as far away as space permitted.

She had a guest room, so if she had wanted to sleep alone, she could have used it. She was here, with him, but the distance between them was some kind of silent commentary.

Offense curled in Zach's belly. He was tired of trying to understand TJ's whims. Tonight had been her doing. He'd come to her house to discuss business, and he would have kept a lid on his own emotions if she hadn't made that impossible.

Working together was also going to be impossible. He wasn't up to TJ's on-again, off-again mood swings. She wanted him, she didn't want him. What the hell did she think he was, some kind of automaton that performed on command?

Zach lay there brooding. TJ was sleeping. The digital clock on the bed stand read 12:33 a.m. He'd really conked out, but he was wide-awake now and should probably get up and go home. He could leave a note and tell TJ thanks for the partnership offer, but the Galaxy was out. It had been an exciting prospect for a few hours, but he didn't have the money to take on a project of that size and complexity. And he wasn't going to let TJ finance all the cost of such extensive expansion. What she needed was a partner who could handle a reasonable share of the expenses, and that sure wasn't him.

As for the two of them, they were better off with the city between them. He would stay on his side of the valley and hope that she stayed on hers. Accidental meetings couldn't be avoided, apparently, but he didn't have to be taken in by soulful gray green eyes.

He'd go to his grave loving this confusing woman, and a part of him would forever speculate about how great a normal relationship with her might have been. So little had been normal for so long. Not since the day he'd faced the harsh facts of Vincent's treachery. Losing everything he'd worked hard to build had been bad enough, but knowing that his own cousin, his only living relative, had deliberately and heartlessly caused it had been an almost lethal blow.

TJ had had it rough, too. Maybe people like them, victims, really, never quite trusted anyone again. In his case he'd had one more blow to absorb, TJ's lack of faith. He hadn't handled that at all well. What good had anger done? He should have calmly sat her down and talked the whole thing out. "If you have some reason to suspect me of such a thing, tell me about it. In detail."

Instead he'd walked out, quit his job. And here he was, back in TJ's bed, so that grand gesture had been nothing but wasted energy.

Zach felt a stinging tightness in his eyes with surprise. Tears? Him? Hell, he hadn't even shed tears when the federal bankruptcy people had padlocked the doors of his business!

There were only a few tears, just enough to remind Zach that he was human and hurting. And that he was tired of everything going to hell in a hand basket. He wanted TJ and he wanted Tina. He wanted a wife he loved and kids to take care of and worry about, a family.

TJ gave only part of herself, the same as he'd done today. His excuse was pride, and he could only guess at hers.

He slid across the big bed. It was funny how priorities and attitudes could slip and slide in the middle of the night, but pride felt only lonely to Zach right now. He wouldn't be in TJ's bed if she hadn't wanted him there, and for her, he fully believed, taking a man to bed meant something.

He didn't intend waking her, but he was driven to lie next to her. She was on her side, facing away from him, and he carefully burrowed his left arm beneath her pillow and laid his right over her waist. They were covered by a sheet and a light blanket, and the bonding of their bare skin created instant electricity.

Her body was like warm satin against his. She hadn't put on a nightgown or pajamas, which was gratifying for Zach. He'd jumped to conclusions again, he realized sadly. Because she hadn't been snuggled up to him when he awoke, he'd immediately assumed her disinterest. Why did that keep happening with them? Why were they both so quick to judge the other?

She felt incredible in his arms, and the inevitable was happening to Zach. Physical response to TJ was automatic for him; be near her and want her.

He thought about getting back on his own side of the bed, but even while debating the point, his hand was moving on her stomach. His insides were getting hot and liquidy. Her round, curving behind fit his lap to perfection. He wanted to explore the beauty of her body, to just lie there and let his fingertips go where they may.

His heart was beating in double time. This was something they hadn't done, one of many, actually. The two times they had made love had been with an almost frantic edge. This was very different from those occasions, with a smoky sensuality Zach found irresistible. His hand crept up to a breast.

He held the soft, arousing mound without movement, basking in the sensation of warm female flesh against his palm. A feeling of love became overwhelming. No other woman would ever replace TJ for him. Marriage had been easy to evade in the past because he hadn't loved any woman with this intensity. He understood it all now, the nonchalance, the relationships he'd enjoyed for a week or a month and then let slip away.

He couldn't let this one vanish, no matter what he had to do to maintain it.

His outlook was ambiguous again, Zach realized. He didn't want to stay on his side of town, not unless TJ was there, too. But how could he agree to a working partnership with his pitiful bank account?

He was getting very aroused, feverish and breathless with desire. Playing around in the dark wasn't a kid's game. Lying curled around TJ and caressing her breasts was sexually thrilling. Her bottom against his lap was eliciting every erotic image in the book. His hand became bolder, sliding down her body and thigh. At her knee, he reversed directions and moved upward, returning to her breasts.

A purring sound from TJ caressed his senses, a sort of low, pleased, "Hmm."

Very tenderly, he rolled a nipple between his thumb and forefinger. Its response was immediate, although he was positive she was still more asleep than awake. Raising his head from the pillow, he peered over her tangle of hair to see her face. Her features were indistinct in the dark, but he could tell that her eyes were closed.

TJ was only partially conscious, floating in a lovely dreamlike state between sleep and wakefulness. Everything was warm and velvety, herself, the bed, the masculine body wrapped around hers. The hand on her breast felt deli-

ciously naughty, the maleness at her back creating ripples of
pleasure.

She liked where she was in that halfway world and made
no attempt to shed its effects. She stirred slightly—lazily,
languorously—aware that Zach's long legs moved when hers
did.

His hand slowly swept downward again. She could feel his
palm, the strangely soft pads of his fingertips on her stomach, her thighs. Deliberately she clung to the haziness of
semiperception; reality could be faced again later, with all
of its cuts and cruelties. This was rare, this was special, and
she wanted it to last as long as possible.

"You're sweet," Zach whispered, so softly TJ could
barely make out the words. Her lips turned up at the corners with the hint of a smile. She was floating on a cloud of
pink cotton candy, half-dreaming, only fractionally aware.

Vaguely she likened his caresses to exploration. He
seemed enthralled with the curves and dips of her body, but
his curiosity kept taking him one step further. He adjusted
their position in subtle ways, very slowly, almost cautiously, as though he didn't want to awaken her fully.

Somehow she was lying more on her back. He'd drawn
her right leg up onto his. She was becoming more alert, she
realized, for the hair on his thighs was quite noticeable
against her smoother skin.

More alert but not less involved, she admitted. He felt
incredible. What he was doing felt incredible. Her temper-
ature was soaring, threatening explosion when he began to
gently tease her most vulnerable spot.

TJ's heart was suddenly thundering in her ears. She was
wide-awake and remembering her decision in the nursery.
She had come back to her own bed, an error in judgment
perhaps, although it hadn't been done carelessly. She'd
thought about spending the night in the guest room and had
consciously chosen not to inflict any more damage on Zach
than would be absolutely necessary to get her point across.
Thus, she'd shed her robe and returned to bed, knowing that

to awaken in the morning alone would undoubtedly hurt Zach.

She hadn't counted on this, probably because it was completely out of the realm of her experience. Even during the first reasonably happy years of their marriage, Tommy had been a man who could sleep through an earthquake. Once out, that was it until morning. TJ couldn't remember ever being awakened in the night to make love.

And that's what Zach wanted, what he was making her want, too. He was a sensual, sensitive man. His touch was tender and arousing, simultaneously.

But they shouldn't make love again until they'd had that vital conversation. Not until she had said what she must and heard from him what was in his heart.

"Zach...wait..." she whispered.

"Wait?"

She had startled him, TJ could tell. Maybe he hadn't even realized that she'd awakened. "We need to talk."

All movement stopped. Zach hesitated, then finally asked, "Do you want a light on?"

The darkness was like a cloak for TJ. Maybe the talk would go better without light, she mused. Maybe they would both feel freer in the dark, less exposed.

It was worth a shot. "No, let's leave the lights off," she said quietly.

They were all entwined, and the idea of disentanglement wasn't very appealing to Zach. But he agreed that they did need to talk. He had reached the end of patience and beating around the bush. He might not have picked this particular moment for a heart-to-heart, but it had to be done and the sooner the better.

Not like this, though. He couldn't talk with any degree of intelligence while he was holding her warm and naked body next to his *hot* and naked body.

He disengaged his arms and legs from hers and moved over a few inches. Then, on impulse, he got off the bed completely, found his briefs where he'd dropped them onto the floor, and yanked them on. Watching his shadowy movements in the dark, TJ's heart was in her throat. Was he angry? Upset?

"Zach, I didn't mean . . ." she began uncertainly.

He interrupted. "It's all right. I just think conversation will come a little easier with some space between us."

"Oh. Well, yes, you're right, of course."

Zach sat on his side of the bed, far enough away from her to avoid contact. "I'll go first," he said bluntly.

He would go first? Had he also been making decisions tonight? She had envisioned laying their situation out from her point of view, then asking for his and hoping the two were reconcilable. Zach's authoritative tone was distressing; she would much rather have been in control of this conversation so that she could steer it in the right direction.

"I thought you were an amazing woman right off the bat. That's the first thing I want you to know," Zach began. "You were doing a terrific job of running your business, and you were alone and pregnant. Those facts kept going through my mind while we talked about everything else. You might not remember, but whenever I got too close to anything personal with you, you backed off."

"I remember." TJ was frowning. Zach going way back to their beginning was disconcerting.

"What you can't possibly know is what I was really feeling for you. Almost immediatley I liked you in a very unprofessional way. It wasn't just ordinary liking, either. I thought of you sexually."

"While I was pregnant?"

"You don't like that idea, do you?"

"It's startling, Zach. I can't help it. I felt very unattractive."

"Well, you weren't. You're quite a woman, TJ. You're bright and intelligent and feminine, and those qualities didn't disappear just because you were carrying a baby. Anyway, one day when I was with you, I thought about marriage. I can't pretend that the idea didn't floor me. It did. I wondered what you'd say and do if I suggested it. I saw your situation as tough, and I wanted to do something for you. To be there for you. To help you any way I could.''

''Zach...''

''Let me finish. I said nothing, but I was caring about you more every day, worrying about you.''

''Oh, Zach,'' she whispered sadly. He was speaking with no holds barred, baring his soul to her, and she hadn't expected such complete candor.

''The day Tina was born felt like a milestone. While I waited, I planned to change things between us. I knew it was up to me to get past our normal working routine. I felt something from you—quite a lot. It gave me hope, anticipation of a future together.

''But I kept putting the big moment off. You were happy at home with Tina and I was busy. Our meetings were the highlight of my days. It all came to a head the day I let you know what was going on in my mind. Your reaction was confusing. I sensed that you felt the same for me as I felt for you, but there was still an invisible barrier, something I couldn't figure out.

''When you finally told me what it was, I couldn't believe it. Out of all the dozens of possibilities, that one knocked me for a loop. I made a bad mistake that day, TJ. We should have had this talk then. Instead of losing my temper and walking out, I should have stayed right here and confronted the problem.

''Now, here it is again, just as traumatic, just as difficult.''

She was nearly frozen in place, hardly daring to breathe throughout his speech, choking on the emotions rushing her. Her voice sounded rusty. ''Do... you love me?''

''Do you want me to love you? You see, TJ, that's what I don't know, what it is you really want?''

''May I explain?''

''Please do.''

TJ drew a long, shaky breath. ''I liked you right away, too. The chemistry I felt with you was... upsetting. I had never been a very sexual person, and I was pregnant and ungainly to boot. I doubt if a man could ever completely comprehend how a woman feels during pregnancy. You're incredibly proud and thrilled with your condition, and at the same time, a little put off by the enormous changes in your appearance. At least I was, although now that I think about it, that attitude wasn't so obvious until you came along. I felt very inadequate, I remember.

"Anyway, I told myself I was imagining things, that you couldn't possibly be attracted to me. A bright, handsome man like you had to have dozens of female friends. Why on earth would you even notice a woman with a forty-inch girth? I blamed my own feelings on confused hormones and did everything I could to ignore them.

"But you were so nice to me, so considerate and thoughtful, and I kept picking up those disturbing messages of physical attraction. I began to wonder why. Why would a man like you go out of your way to be so kind to a woman who waddled when she walked?"

Zach couldn't help laughing, although TJ was undoubtedly serious. "It might be funny now," she said with some grimness, "but it wasn't then."

"I know. Go on."

"What could you want from me, I kept asking myself. I was denying any possibility of a normal physical attraction. In the first place, I didn't even understand that kind of relationship. My one and only experience with a man was with Tommy, and he was kind only when he wanted something."

"So you looked for some devious reason for my attentions and you found one," Zach interjected flatly.

"Yes, the business. I deplored the idea, Zach. I fought it," she said passionately, then sighed. "It wouldn't leave me be. I'm more ashamed of that than anything else I've ever done. But the year had been so...exhausting."

"For me, too."

"Yes, for you, too. Zach, we met at a bad time for both of us. Neither of us was over the shock of the past. It takes longer than a few months to heal a really deep wound, and yours was dreadfully deep.''

"So was yours. I hadn't guessed, you know. I wondered why there weren't any signs of Tommy in this house, not even a picture.''

"I have them, Zach. Pictures, mementos, some personal things. They're packed away for Tina. She'll want to know about her father someday.''

"Yes, I'm sure she will.''

TJ licked her dry lips. The next phase of this conversation was the most crucial. Zach did care about her. He was physically attracted to her, or he wouldn't be here. But she wasn't certain that his feelings went beyond caring and desire.

And hers did.

She was glad they hadn't turned on a light. Their voices had sounded muted and, for the most part, unemotional. Zach was a shadowy form sitting on the bed. The bedroom door was slightly ajar and the dim glow from the nursery couldn't begin to penetrate the room's darkness.

Secrets in the dark, TJ thought. That's what was happening. They were opening their hearts and exchanging their most private thoughts and feelings.

"You said you didn't know what I want," she said softly. "It's really very simple, Zach. I said it in the kitchen. I love you. I think I've loved you all along. I've been very foolish with you, and I pray that that foolishness hasn't destroyed every chance we had.''

Zach's heart began beating very hard. "TJ, are you sure?''

"Very sure. I've missed you terribly. I debated about calling you for weeks before I got up the nerve.''

"And I cut you cold.''

"You hadn't forgiven me.''

"I took out the entire year's anguish on you.''

"Maybe. And maybe I transferred all of the mistrust and uncertainty I'd endured with Tommy to you. I know my reactions to you were influenced by my marriage.''

"Probably."

TJ chewed on her bottom lip. He still hadn't said he loved her. Did he? Could she bear it if he didn't? It was up to him now. She had no secrets left, nothing remaining in her soul that he didn't know.

Zach pulled back the sheet and blanket, and TJ's heart leaped into her throat. He stood up, shed his briefs and crawled back into bed. Then he was beside her, gathering her to himself. His arms were around her, her head on his chest, his lips in her hair. "I told myself I could forget you," he whispered. "But I couldn't. I told myself that I didn't love you, that it wouldn't matter if I never saw you again. More lies. TJ, I do love you. I think I always have."

Tears filled her eyes. "I love you so much."

"No more than I love you." He knew she was weeping quietly, and he held her and felt the same strong emotion tugging at him. "I want the best for us," he whispered raggedly.

"The best," she agreed on a sob.

"TJ..."

"Yes?"

"About the Galaxy...I don't think it would be the wisest move for me to make."

"You don't?" She raised her head, attempting to see his eyes in the dark.

"I'm just getting started again, and I don't have the means to finance the cost of the kind of expansion the Galaxy would require. And please don't say that you'll take care of finances. Getting my business off the ground is something I have to do myself."

TJ was silent a moment. She understood his attitude, but there was something else that needed discussion, a hope, an idea that had been developing all on its own. After her ghastly display of mistrust before, Zach might think she'd lost her mind.

But it was so important, such a beautiful dream.

And she wanted to see his face while she told him about it. Scooting away, TJ switched on the bedside lamp. Zach sat up, blinking at the sudden infusion of light. "What's wrong?" he questioned.

"I need to tell you something." He looked slightly wary again. "You might not like it," she warned. "But I'm hoping you'll at least consider it."

"Is it about the Galaxy?"

"It's mostly about me." The bedding was tangled around them, and TJ was holding an edge of the sheet to her breasts. "It's a dream I have, Zach, one that was born when Tina was. I didn't realize it at first, not until I was home and caring for her."

She took a deep breath. "Zach, I don't want to run the business anymore."

He did a classic double take. "You don't want to what?"

"Run the business. I want to stay home and take care of Tina. At least until she starts school. If we formed that partnership with our companies, there'd only be one to run. And you could do it."

"TJ!" He looked so startled, TJ almost laughed.

"Zach, it's so perfect. You love the construction business. I used to, but that's all I had. Now I've got Tina and you and so many better ideas about how to spend my time."

Zach lay back against the pillows, totally astounded. "You never cease to amaze me," he exclaimed. "TJ, I can't just take over your business. What would people think?"

"People? What people?"

"Everyone! Doreen, Jim, the rest of the employees, people in the trade, everyone you deal with! Everyone *I* deal with."

"I really don't care what anyone else thinks, do you?" When he didn't immediately agree, TJ sighed and then had to bat her eyelashes to keep some sudden tears at bay.

Zach studied her. "We have a bigger problem than that, honey," he said softly, and wiped at an escaping tear beneath TJ's left eye.

"We do?" she quavered.

"How does a man with very few assets ask the woman he loves to marry him when the lady in question already has everything that the guy's working to attain?"

TJ gulped a throatful of salty tears and moaned, "Don't look at it that way, please!" She tried to laugh. "If that was a proposal, I accept. I should have said yes the first time you talked about marriage."

"Maybe, maybe not." Zach lay back, crooking his arm beneath his head. "The time wasn't right then, TJ."

"But it is now. What difference does it make who owns what? I won't listen to that, Zach. Do you have any idea what you and I being here together and admitting love for one another means to me?"

Zach cast probing eyes on her. "You can't turn your back on public opinion, TJ."

"Oh, yes, I can!"

She sounded stubbornly entrenched in that attitude. Her determination touched Zach, but he saw himself as a little more realistic about the matter. "And you'd like to quit working and just turn everything over to me."

"Yes."

"Indefinitely?"

"Until our...children are older, yes. Then I'll probably want to get involved again."

He couldn't help smiling. She was talking about children as though they already had a houseful, when only one tiny baby resided in the nursery.

"I thought you were completely dedicated to your business," he said thoughtfully.

"I was. And if you refuse, I'll have to keep on going to work every morning and leaving Tina with Daisy. And even if I managed to convince you to marry me, another baby would be very impractical. Zach, I want another baby, *your* baby."

He put his hand on her cheek and tenderly caressed it. "Your arguments are pretty hard to combat."

"Don't combat them. We could have everything. We've already *got* everything. It just needs a little rearranging. And

I'm deadly serious about not giving two hoots about what anyone else might think about you and me merging our companies into one operation. I know what kind of man you are, and I know that you'll make more of a success with the business than I could in a million years.''

"Well, I don't know about that," he said wryly. "You've done well, TJ. That's one argument that won't sway me."

"Then I won't use it." TJ dropped the sheet, leaned over him and put her arms around his neck. "But how about this one?" She seductively rubbed her breasts against his chest while fitting her mouth to his. His arms went around her while a masculine growl of pure pleasure welled in his throat.

"That one might work," he said thickly when they broke apart for air. His hands swept down her back and urged her hips on top of his. "This one might work even better," he whispered as he slid into the heat of her body. "Oh, baby, this one will work for sure," he groaned.

TJ was out of bed at Tina's first wail. Grabbing her robe, she glanced at the clock: 5:14 a.m. The little darling had slept through the night again and was probably ravenously hungry.

"TJ?" Zach said drowsily.

"Go back to sleep, darling. I'm going to get Tina a bottle."

He sat up. "I'll help."

TJ grinned. "Fine. You can pick her up and hold her while I get the bottle ready."

Zach got out of bed and pulled on his jeans. While TJ headed for the kitchen, he went to the nursery. "Hey, hey, what's all the fuss about?" he said soothingly, and reached for the tiny girl in the crib.

She was waving her little fists and kicking up an awful racket. Zach laughed softly and picked her up. Then he frowned. She was soaked clear through. "Hey, punkin, I understand now. I'd yell, too, if I was that wet."

He glanced around. A stack of diapers was on a shelf, which was one question answered. As for a fresh nightgown, he'd probably find one in that bureau.

Carrying Tina, who had quietened only slightly, he gathered up a diaper and a clean nightgown. Then he brought the whole armful across the hall to TJ's bed.

When TJ returned with a warm bottle, she stood in the doorway for a moment to absorb the scene. Zach was struggling with the clean diaper and a wriggling, screaming Tina. "Take it easy, punkin," he was pleading. "Mama's coming any second now with your breakfast. Give me a minute to figure this thing out, and you'll be dry and comfy again."

She loved this man more than life itself, TJ thought, nearly melting at the sight of him trying to comfort her baby.

Quickly then, she went to rescue Zach. "Here, hold the bottle," she told him when Tina's little mouth had clamped around the nipple. Deftly TJ got the baby out of her wet clothes and into the dry things.

Her eyes met Zach's over the greedily suckling infant. "This is what I want," she said emotionally. "You and Tina and at least one more baby. A family, Zach. A husband I adore and beautiful babies. What else could possibly compare with that?"

Zach felt tears searing his eyes. TJ and babies. The woman he loved, a family, *his* family. TJ was right and he was wrong. What did anyone else's opinion matter? What did pride matter? He knew his own capabilities, and he knew that he'd work his tail off at whatever job he was doing.

He cleared his throat. "I love you, TJ. Will you marry me?"

Tears filled her eyes. "Yes," she whispered. "Oh, yes." Tina was in her arms, but she leaned forward to kiss the man she loved so much. Zach's lips met hers over the baby, and then they sat back and grinned at each other.

"We need a name for the new company," TJ murmured.

" 'Reese Home Builders' is too established to put aside, TJ."

"Then, how about Torelli-Reese? I want to announce to the whole world that we've joined forces, Zach. Permanently."

He laughed. "Well, that would do it, all right."

TJ's smile turned teasing. "Did you believe me when I told you yesterday that my intentions were strictly business?"

"I think you believed it at the time."

"I did, but did you?"

Zach moved closer and wrapped his arms around both mother and daughter. "I don't think it was 'strictly business' for you and me from the moment I walked into your office looking for a job."

TJ smiled contentedly. "You're sure right about that, my love."

* * * * *

The spirit of motherhood is the spirit of love—and how better to capture that special feeling than in our short story collection...

to Mother with Love '92

Curtiss Ann Matlock
Carole Halston
Linda Shaw

Three glorious new stories that embody the very essence of family and romance are contained in this heartfelt tribute to Mother. Share in the joy by joining us and three of your favorite Silhouette authors for this celebration of motherhood and romance.

Available at your favorite retail outlet in May.

SMD92

® **SILHOUETTE**® *Desire*™

MAN OF THE MONTH

WHERE THERE IS LOVE

Annette Broadrick

Secret agent Max Moran knew all too well the rules of a road where life-threatening danger lurked around every corner. He stalked his prey like a panther—silent, stealthy and ready to spring at any moment.

But teaming up again with delicate, determined Marisa Stevens meant tackling a far more tortuous terrain—one that Max had spent a lifetime avoiding. This precariously unpredictable path was enough to break the stoic panther's stride...as it wove its way to where there was love.

Last sighted in CANDLELIGHT FOR TWO (Silhouette Desire #577), the mysterious Max is back as Silhouette's *Man of the Month!* Don't miss Max's story, WHERE THERE IS LOVE by Annette Broadrick, available in May...only from Silhouette Desire.

SDAB

FREE GIFT OFFER

To receive your free gift, send us the specified number of proofs-of-purchase from any specially marked Free Gift Offer Harlequin or Silhouette book with the Free Gift Certificate properly completed, plus a check or money order (do not send cash) to cover postage and handling payable to Harlequin/Silhouette Free Gift Promotion Offer. We will send you the specified gift.

FREE GIFT CERTIFICATE

ITEM	A. GOLD TONE EARRINGS	B. GOLD TONE BRACELET	C. GOLD TONE NECKLACE
# of proofs-of-purchase required	3	6	9
Postage and Handling	$1.75	$2.25	$2.75
Check one	☐	☐	☐

Name: _____

Address: _____

City: _____ State: _____ Zip Code: _____

Mail this certificate, specified number of proofs-of-purchase and a check or money order for postage and handling to: HARLEQUIN/SILHOUETTE FREE GIFT OFFER 1992, P.O. Box 9057, Buffalo, NY 14269-9057. Requests must be received by July 31, 1992.

PLUS—Every time you submit a completed certificate with the correct number of proofs-of-purchase, you are automatically entered in our MILLION DOLLAR SWEEPSTAKES! No purchase or obligation necessary to enter. See below for alternate means of entry and how to obtain complete sweepstakes rules.

MILLION DOLLAR SWEEPSTAKES
NO PURCHASE OR OBLIGATION NECESSARY TO ENTER

To enter, hand-print (mechanical reproductions are not acceptable) your name and address on a 3"×5" card and mail to Million Dollar Sweepstakes 6097, c/o either P.O. Box 9056, Buffalo, NY 14269-9056 or P.O. Box 621, Fort Erie, Ontario L2A 5X3. Limit: one entry per envelope. Entries must be sent via 1st-class mail. For eligibility, entries must be received no later than March 31, 1994. No liability is assumed for printing errors, lost, late or misdirected entries.

Sweepstakes is open to persons 18 years of age or older. All applicable laws and regulations apply. Sweepstakes offer void wherever prohibited by law. Prizewinners will be determined no later than May 1994. Chances of winning are determined by the number of entries distributed and received. For a copy of the Official Rules governing this sweepstakes offer, send a self-addressed, stamped envelope (WA residents need not affix return postage) to: Million Dollar Sweepstakes Rules, P.O. Box 4733, Blair, NE 68009.

SD1U

 ONE PROOF-OF-PURCHASE
To collect your fabulous FREE GIFT you must include the necessary FREE GIFT proofs-of-purchase with a properly completed offer certificate.

(See center insert for details)